EXTRACTS

English Fiction for Advanced Students

Nelson

Nigel Newbrook

For
Neil and Ralph

With Special Thanks To

Jacky Newbrook

for typing the original draft, and for
her constructive comments, which especially
contributed to the final format of the units.

Thomas Nelson and Sons Ltd
Nelson House   Mayfield Road
Walton-on-Thames   Surrey
KT12 5PL   UK

51 York Place
Edinburgh
EH1 3JD   UK

Thomas Nelson (Hong Kong) Ltd
Toppan Building 10/F
22A Westlands Road
Quarry Bay   Hong Kong

© Nigel Newbrook 1989

First published by Thomas Nelson and Sons Ltd 1989

ISBN 0–17–555728–4

NPN 9 8 7 6 5 4 3 2 1

Acknowledgements

Texts
The publishers are grateful to the following for permission to reproduce copyright material: Everyman's Library, J. M. Dent for the extract from *The Woman in White* by Wilkie Collins; A. P. Watt Ltd. on behalf of The Literary Executors of the Estate of H. G. Wells for the extract from *The First Men in the Moon*; Edward Arnold Ltd. for the extract from *A Room with a View* by E. M. Forster; The Estate of the Late Sonia Brownell Orwell and Secker & Warburg Ltd. for the extract from *1984* by George Orwell; Faber and Faber Ltd. for the extract from *Lord of the Flies* by William Golding; Eyre & Spottiswode for the extract from *Room at the Top* by John Braine; William Heinemann Ltd. for the extract from *The Jewel in the Crown* by Paul Scott; Jonathan Cape Ltd. for the extract from *Hotel du Lac* by Anita Brookner; *The Daily Mail* for the extract from the front page 21 July 1969; Associated Newspapers for the extract from the front page of *The Evening News* 21 July 1969; *The Evening Standard* for the extract from the front page 19 October 1987; *The Independent* for the extract from the front page 20 October 1987; The Tobacco Advisory Council for its advertisement and the extract contained therein © Today Newspaper; The Health Education Authority for its advertisement.

Photographs
The publishers wish to thank the following for permission to reproduce copyright photographs: Colonel Lane Fox (the portrait of Marcia Fox by Sir William Beechey hangs in the Gallery at Bramham Park, near Wetherby, West Yorkshire) p1; BBC Hulton Library pp 5, 9, 13, 21, 37; S & R Greenhill pp 9, 17 left, centre, right; Thomas Nelson and Sons Ltd. p 17; Ed Barber pp 13, 25; Co. Graf S.r.l. p 33; Casa Editrice Giusti de Becocci p 33; L. H. Hurrel (The Mayflower by Bernard Gribble is on loan to the Plymouth Museum and Art Gallery) p 45; Sporting Pictures UK Ltd. p 49 top left, top right; Rex Features Ltd. p 49, centre left & right, bottom left & right; The National Gallery (The Fighting Temeraire by W. S. Turner) p 53; J. Allan Cash p 57.
Every effort has been made to trace owners of the copyright, but if any omissions can be rectified the publishers will be pleased to make the necessary arrangements.

Contents

TEACHER'S INTRODUCTION

Aims of the book

The main purpose of the book is to introduce foreign students to some of the major works of English fiction in a clear, straightforward way, whilst providing the chance to practise reading skills at the advanced level. This practice is especially useful for those students aiming to take the Cambridge Certificate of Proficiency in English examination (C.P.E.). Related exercises also provide the opportunity for oral practice, summary and composition writing, and vocabulary work.

How the book is organised

There are fifteen units, based around fifteen novels taken in chronological order, with a separate introductory background section on the writers in the same order.

Each unit is based around a theme arising from the selected text. The book can therefore be used in two ways:
- a) chronologically: i.e. the teacher follows the order of the units. This is especially recommended for teachers of literature classes;
- b) thematically: i.e. the teacher selects units depending on the choice of themes. This may be preferred in general language classes, especially if a thematic approach is being used in class.

Either approach would be equally successful, since the units are self-contained, and are not arranged in order of difficulty. There is an answer section at the back of the book.

How the units are organised

There are seven sections in each unit, consisting of:
1. visual or textual prompts and discussion points, as 'pre-reading' activities;
2. a short paragraph setting the context of the selected text (sometimes with a contemporary or relevant illustration);
3. the text itself;
4. comprehension and appreciation questions, plus a summary exercise related to C.P.E. Paper 3 Section B. It is recommended that the questions are looked at before the text is read, thereby providing a 'while-reading' activity, in addition to the more obvious 'post-reading' one in which the questions are actually answered;
5. vocabulary work, often involving phrasal verbs or idioms;
6. a short role-play section, involving discussion of a point arising from one aspect of the materials in the unit;
7. a composition topic, similar to those set in C.P.E. Paper 2.

What each section contains

1 The visual or textual prompts and the discussion points provide a pre-reading activity; getting the students to start thinking of the central theme and anticipating various aspects of it should assist their eventual reading of the text.

Teachers need not necessarily use all the discussion points suggested, and may like to add some of their own.

These points could be discussed by the class as a whole, or by smaller groups, who could then report back to the others on their opinions. This could also be done as a 'jigsaw activity'; students could be in groups A, B, and C for the initial discussion, and then regrouped into groups 1, 2 and 3 (each containing students from the original A, B and C), as shown below:

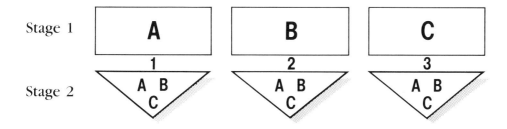

This would then provide an exchange of information activity.

2 It is most important that the students understand the context of the selected extract, so the teacher should check this carefully, either by direct questions, or a short discussion. This will facilitate comprehension of the text.

3 Students will appreciate a clear and lively reading, giving appropriate stress, either by the teacher him/herself, or pre-recorded on a cassette tape if preferred. This will also help the students' comprehension of the text. As stated earlier, teachers should go through the questions in Section 4 first, in order to provide a focus for the students whilst the reading is taking place.

4 The questions could either be answered:
   a) as homework (but remember there are answers in the back!)
   b) by the students working individually in class
   c) by the students working in pairs or small groups in class.
The three alternatives could be used as follows:
   a) to encourage self-study
   b) to provide 'mock exam' practice (if so, a maximum of 30 minutes should be allowed)
   c) to promote interaction and communication
Teachers may decide to vary their approach from unit to unit, depending on their requirements, or to provide variety. Alternative (c) could also be done as a 'jigsaw activity' (as explained in Section 1). If so, answers could be compared in stage 2, generating further discussion, if there are differences of opinion.

Whichever approach is adopted, students should always be encouraged to look out for inferences and implications, to try to deduce meaning, and also to try and see the writer's purpose in the choice of words used, which may be to convey a certain tone (e.g. sarcasm).

5   The three approaches suggested above could also be used in relation to the exercises in this section. Occasionally, they could be done at the end of the lesson as a team quiz; students often find this an enjoyable way to finish the lesson.

Some of the vocabulary exercises are intended to provide the opportunity for further practice of phrasal verbs and idioms. Others are intended to extend the students' grasp of vocabulary by focussing attention on the connotations of a word, and on words that are close, but different, in meaning, or that differ in intensity. Some exercises focus attention on particular words from the selected text, and one deals with the use of foreign expressions in English.

6   These suggestions for role-play activities are only intended to provide a short, oral activity based around a point arising from materials in the unit. The role-plays do not involve an 'information gap'; students should therefore read both role descriptions. The roles either place the student in the exact situation of the text, and ask him/her to be one of the characters, or else they involve a situation in a modern-day context related to one aspect of the unit.

7   Each unit contains a composition topic similar to the kind set in C.P.E. Paper 2. The main range of different topics offered in the exam paper (descriptive, discursive, narrative or task-based) is covered over the fifteen units of the book. However, there are no 'set book' questions, since the students have only read extracts and not complete novels.

Teachers will probably want to set these compositions for homework, but may find it useful to have a short, general discussion beforehand, to get students thinking of the subject matter. Students should also be encouraged to do an outline plan first, before writing the composition itself.

Related work

Teachers may like to encourage students to read the complete novel, once the extract has been studied, and/or another book by the same author, depending on student interest. This could form the basis of a mini-project, which could be done either individually or in pairs or small groups. The aim might be to write a book review, give a report to the class on the book as a whole, or show how the theme of the extract is developed throughout the book. Students interested in drama might like to write and act out short scenes based on central parts of the novel, using modern English.

Note about the units

a) The order of the sections in Unit 11 has been slightly changed to maintain a logical progression throughout the unit.

b) Units 9 and 15, whilst basically self-contained, both concern events at hotels. The composition topic in Unit 15 refers to the hotel in Unit 9, although this would not necessarily prevent the composition being written solely on a reading of Unit 15. However, teachers working thematically may like to link these two units, since they both call for responses to different types of hotels and holidays.

BACKGROUND TO THE AUTHORS AND EXTRACTS

Unit 1   *Emma* by Jane Austen *(Published in 1816)*

The early English novelists are usually considered to be Daniel Defoe (1660–1731), Samuel Richardson (1689–1761) and Henry Fielding (1707–1754). However, Jane Austen (1775–1817) brought the novel to the form we recognise today. She is concerned with everyday life situations, and both character and plot develop as the novel progresses. Her writing is sometimes referred to as 'a comedy of manners', since she portrayed in a humorous manner the behaviour of middle-class families in the Regency period (1812–1820).

Unit 2   *Wuthering Heights* by Emily Brontë *(Published in 1847)*

The three Brontë Sisters, Charlotte (1816–1855), Emily (1818–1848), and Anne (1820–1849), lived in the small village of Haworth on the Yorkshire moors, where their father was the rector of the local church. The girls spent a lot of time by themselves, reading and writing and telling stories. Charlotte's famous novel is *Jane Eyre*, and Anne wrote *The Tenant of Wildfell Hall*. *Wuthering Heights* is Emily's masterpiece, which is set on the wild and desolate Yorkshire moors.

Unit 3   *Vanity Fair* by William Makepeace Thackeray *(Published in 1847–48)*

Thackeray (1811–1863) was the son of an official of the British East India Company, and was educated at a famous public school and Cambridge University. He loved writing, and contributed many humorous, and often satirical articles to various literary magazines. *Vanity Fair*, published in monthly parts (like Dickens's novels) made him really famous and is considered his greatest work. Thackeray's plots tended to be more true to life than some of the melodramatic ones of his contemporaries. He felt the novelist had the right to moralise to the reader, and intersperses his narrative with comment on human behaviour, especially criticising hypocrisy, vanity and snobbery.

Unit 4   *The Woman in White* by Wilkie Collins *(Published in 1860)*

Wilkie Collins (1824–1889) was the son of a landscape painter. He worked in the tea trade before qualifying as a lawyer, but he was always more interested in writing, painting and acting. He is now recognised as one of the first authors to write mystery stories, and is most well-known for *The Woman in White* and *The Moonstone*. He was a friend of Charles Dickens, and they often acted together in amateur theatrical productions.

Unit 5 *Great Expectations* by Charles Dickens *(Published in 1860–61)*

Charles Dickens (1812–1870) was the most famous novelist in the Victorian period (1837–1901), when the British Empire was at its height, and Britain was the most prosperous industrial nation in the world.

However, the wealth and high standard of living of the upper classes were dependent on the hard work of the lower classes. Men, women and children worked long hours in the coal mines, cotton mills and factories, and families lived in squalid houses, crammed together in the industrial areas, with no proper sanitation. Some of these conditions are described by Dickens in *Oliver Twist* and *Hard Times*, and the source of wealth is a symbolic theme in his later novels, *Great Expectations* and *Our Mutual Friend*.

Great Expectations is considered to be Dickens's most technically perfect novel.

Unit 6 *Silas Marner* by George Eliot *(Published in 1861)*

George Eliot (1819–1880) was the pen-name of Mary Ann Evans, which she used in order that her work should be taken seriously. She spent her early years in the countryside in Warwickshire, and this gave her the knowledge of the everyday life of ordinary people, which plays a central part in her novels. In *Silas Marner*, in particular, she paints a vivid picture of what village life was like at the start of the nineteenth century (when this story takes place).

Unit 7 *The Return of the Native* by Thomas Hardy *(Published in 1878)*

Thomas Hardy (1840–1928) is famous for his novels portraying country life in the south-west of England, which he called 'Wessex'. These novels show the changing times in the countryside, as the old way of life is gradually taken over by industrialization. They are often pessimistic, revealing Hardy's sense of the inevitable tragedy of human life, as is often demonstrated by Hardy's use of fatal coincidences and misunderstandings.

Unit 8 *The First Men in the Moon* by H. G. Wells *(Published in 1901)*

H. G. Wells (1866–1946) is famous for his science-fiction stories foretelling future scientific inventions. He was a shopkeeper's son who eventually won a scholarship to study at what is now the Imperial College of Science in London. He became increasingly concerned with the dangers which lay in technological developments, and the outbreak of the Second World War convinced him that mankind had finally lost control over the forces it had created. His other famous novels are *The Time Machine*, *The Invisible Man* and *The War of the Worlds*.

Unit 9   *A Room With a View* by E. M. Forster *(Published in 1908)*

E. M. Forster (1879–1910) had an upper middle class upbringing, and went to public school and Cambridge University. Four of his five novels were published in the period prior to the First World War, and are partly a comment on the social life of his class at the time, both at home and abroad. Personal relations are always important in his work, as is the problem of communication between different cultures and civilizations. His novels are written in a much more natural and colloquial style than those of the late nineteenth century.

Unit 10   *Sons and Lovers* by D. H. Lawrence *(Published in 1913)*

D. H. Lawrence (1885–1930) was the son of a coal-miner and grew up in the mining area of Nottinghamshire. His mother had been a teacher and had encouraged her son to have higher ambitions than to work in the local pit. He won a scholarship to Nottingham High School and, after going to university, became a teacher in London.

His novels show a concern for natural feelings and emotions and a dislike for the way modern industry destroys the basic, primitive qualities of life. *Sons and Lovers* is partly autobiographical, based on his upbringing and relationship with his parents, especially his mother.

Unit 11   *1984* by George Orwell *(Published in 1949)*

George Orwell (1903–1950) is the pen-name of Eric Blair, who was born in Bengal, the son of a British official in the Indian Civil Service. He attended Eton College, and worked for a time in the Indian Police, but began to resent imperialism and the fact that he was unable to mix with the local people. Consequently, he returned to Europe and lived for some time among the poor people of London and Paris. He was strongly against any kind of authoritarian government, as can be seen in his two most famous works, *Animal Farm* and *1984*.

Unit 12   *Lord of the Flies* by William Golding *(Published in 1954)*

William Golding (born in 1911) was educated at Oxford University and became a teacher. He served in the Royal Navy in the Second World War, and returned to teaching until becoming a full-time writer. His novels often reveal his interest in the nature and power of evil, and in 1983 he won the Nobel Prize for Literature for the way in which his writing deals with the human condition. *Lord of the Flies*, written in 1954 and made into a successful film in 1963, is possibly his most famous work, although a later novel, *Rites of Passage*, won the Booker McConnell Prize in 1980.

Unit 13 *Room at the Top* by John Braine (*Published in 1957*)

Writers in Britain in the late 1950s are often referred to as 'the angry young men'. (This is partly associated with John Osborne's play *Look Back in Anger* which was first produced in 1956.) They dealt with working class people who were dissatisfied with the class structure and their position in society. John Braine (born in 1922) was working as a librarian in Yorkshire when *Room at the Top* brought him instant fame. It quickly became a bestseller and was also made into a successful film.

Unit 14 *The Jewel in the Crown* by Paul Scott (*Published in 1966*)

Paul Scott (1920–1978) is particularly well-known for his novels about life in India, where he served in the army in the Second World War. In 1963 he was elected a Fellow of the Royal Society of Literature, and in 1977 he won the Booker McConnell Prize for his novel *Staying On*. The novel *The Jewel in the Crown* is actually the first part of *The Raj Quartet*, the other three novels being *The Day of the Scorpion*, *The Towers of Silence* and *A Division of the Spoils*. Together they cover the last five years of British rule in India.

Unit 15 *Hotel du Lac* by Anita Brookner (*Published in 1984*)

Anita Brookner was educated at the University of London, and at the Courtauld Institute, Paris. She is now an international authority on eighteenth- and nineteenth-century paintings, and has been Reader at the Courtauld Institute of Art since 1977. In addition to writing about art, she has written several novels including *A Start in Life*, *Providence*, *Hotel du Lac* (which won the Booker McConnell Prize in 1984), and *Latecomers* (published in 1988).

Unit 1 SELFISHNESS

Emma by Jane Austen
(1816)

'All sensible people are selfish' Ralph Waldo Emerson (1803–1882)

Discussion

- To what extent might it be sensible to be selfish? Give examples of particular instances or occasions.
- What examples of behaviour would you regard as 'selfish' in a negative sense?
- How would you deal with a friend who had selfish tendencies?

The Novel

Jane Austen's most well-known novel *Pride and Prejudice* (1813), centres around the relationship between Elizabeth Bennet and Mr Darcy. *Emma* is her most highly acclaimed work, however, and can be regarded as her technical masterpiece. It concerns Emma Woodhouse, who has every advantage in life and is used to organising the lives of others, getting her own way, and believing she is always in the right.

EMMA WOODHOUSE, handsome, clever, and rich, with a comfortable home and happy disposition, seemed to unite some of the best blessings of existence; and had lived nearly twenty-one years in the world with very little to distress or vex her.

5   She was the youngest of the two daughters of a most affectionate, indulgent father, and had, in consequence of her sister's marriage, been mistress of his house from a very early period. Her mother had died too long ago for her to have more than an indistinct remembrance of her caresses, and her place had been supplied by an excellent woman as governess, who had fallen little short of a
10 mother in affection.

    Sixteen years had Miss Taylor been in Mr Woodhouse's family, less as a governess than a friend, very fond of both daughters, but particularly of Emma. Between *them* it was more the intimacy of sisters. Even before Miss Taylor had ceased to hold the nominal office of governess, the mildness of her temper had
15 hardly allowed her to impose any restraint; and the shadow of authority being now long passed away, they had been living together as friend and friend very mutually attached, and Emma doing just what she liked; highly esteeming Miss Taylor's judgment, but directed chiefly by her own.

    The real evils indeed of Emma's situation were the power of having rather
20 too much her own way, and a disposition to think a little too well of herself; these were the disadvantages which threatened alloy to her many enjoyments. The danger, however, was at present so unperceived, that they did not by any means rank as misfortunes with her.

    Sorrow came – a gentle sorrow – but not at all in the shape of any
25 disagreeable consciousness. – Miss Taylor married. It was Miss Taylor's loss which first brought grief. It was on the wedding-day of this beloved friend that Emma first sat in mournful thought of any continuance. The wedding over and the bride-people gone, her father and herself were left to dine together, with no prospect of a third to cheer a long evening. Her father composed himself to sleep
30 after dinner, as usual, and she had then only to sit and think of what she had lost.

    The event had every promise of happiness for her friend. Mr Weston was a man of unexceptionable character, easy fortune, suitable age and pleasant manners; and there was some satisfaction in considering with what self-
35 denying, generous friendship she had always wished and promoted the match; but it was a black morning's work for her. The want of Miss Taylor would be felt every hour of every day. She recalled her past kindness – the kindness, the affection of sixteen years – how she had taught and how she had played with her

from five years old – how she had devoted all her powers to attach and amuse
40 her in health – and how nursed her through the various illnesses of childhood. A
large debt of gratitude was owing here; but the intercourse of the last seven
years, the equal footing and perfect unreserve which had soon followed
Isabella's marriage on their being left to each other, was yet a dearer, tenderer
recollection. It had been a friend and companion such as few possessed,
45 intelligent, well-informed, useful, gentle, knowing all the ways of the family,
interested in all its concerns, and peculiarly interested in herself, in every
pleasure, every scheme of her's; – one to whom she could speak every thought as
it arose, and who had such an affection for her as could never find fault.

How was she to bear the change? – It was true that her friend was going only
50 half a mile from them; but Emma was aware that great must be the difference
between a Mrs Weston only half a mile from them, and a Miss Taylor in the
house; and with all her advantages, natural and domestic, she was now in great
danger of suffering from intellectual solitude. She dearly loved her father, but
he was no companion for her. He could not meet her in conversation, rational or
55 playful.

alloy (21): something that lowers the quality of the thing to which it is added.

Understanding and Appreciating

1   Explain why Emma had been 'mistress of his house' from an early age (lines
6–7).
2   Who does the word 'them' refer to in line 13?
3   Why is Miss Taylor's role as governess referred to as 'nominal' (line 14)?
4   Explain in your own words what the 'disadvantages' were that threatened to
spoil Emma's enjoyment (line 21).
5   How does Jane Austen's use of vocabulary in lines 24–27 show that Emma
sees the wedding more in terms of a sadder ceremony?
6   What kind of character do you expect Mr Weston to have from the use of
'unexceptionable' (line 33)?
7   What had made the 'last seven years' of Emma's relationship with Miss Taylor
so special?
8   What do you understand to be the difference between 'a Mrs Weston only
half a mile from them, and a Miss Taylor in the house' (lines 51–52)?

Summary Writing

In a short paragraph of 60–80 words, summarise (in your own words) Miss
Taylor's behaviour towards Emma over the previous sixteen years.

Vocabulary

Discuss the following adjectives with a partner, and decide whether they indicate positive or negative characteristics, or are neutral. (There may be different views on some qualities!) The first four adjectives come from the text.

affectionate, indulgent, generous, gentle, sarcastic, sympathetic, vindictive, self-effacing, sensitive. e a

Positive	Negative	Neutral

Idioms

Match the idioms, based on colours, on the left with the correct definition on the right. (The first one comes from the text.)

1   a black morning's work
2   to be black and blue
3   to blackmail someone
4   a red-letter day
5   to see red
6   to be in the red
7   to feel blue
8   a blue-print

a   to become angry
b   a detailed plan
c   to be depressed
d   to owe the bank money
e   to be very bruised
f   a very important day
g   to have done something which had sad results
h   to obtain money by threatening to reveal discreditable secrets

Role-play (Pairwork)

Student A: you are Miss Taylor. Explain to Emma that Mr Weston has asked you to marry him, and that you will have to leave soon.
Student B: you are Emma. Express your disappointment, and try to see how far Miss Weston has thought through what she is going to do.

Composition

Describe your best friend. (About 350 words.)

Unit 2 DISAPPOINTMENT

Wuthering Heights by Emily Brontë (1847)

... Well, first of all it turned out that he hadn't got a car, so we had to go into town by bus. Then we only had chicken and chips in a pub instead of the promised three-course dinner at the new restaurant! To cap it all, we spent the rest of the evening at that broken-down old local cinema, instead of going to see Pavarotti at the Opera House!

Discussion

- Who is this letter from, and to?
- What would you have done in this situation?
- Can you remember a particularly disappointing incident in your childhood?

The Novel

The story is told (after it has happened) by Nelly Dean, the housekeeper, to Mr Lockwood, the new tenant of Thrushcross Grange. It concerns two families, the Lintons (of Thrushcross Grange) and the Earnshaws (of Wuthering Heights), and an outsider called Heathcliff.

The main plot concerns the obsessive love of Heathcliff and Catherine Earnshaw. Despite being in love with him, she marries Edgar Linton because she feels a marriage to Heathcliff would degrade her. After her death, Heathcliff attempts to avenge himself on the Linton family. In this extract Nelly Dean recalls the day Heathcliff was first brought home by Catherine's father, Mr Earnshaw.

One fine summer morning – it was the beginning of harvest, I remember –
Mr Earnshaw, the old master, came down stairs, dressed for a journey; and,
after he had told Joseph what was to be done during the day, he turned to
Hindley and Cathy, and me – for I sat eating my porridge, with them – and he
5   said, speaking to his son,
'Now, my bonny man, I'm going to Liverpool to-day . . . What shall I bring
you? You may choose what you like; only let it be little, for I shall walk there and
back; sixty miles each way, that is a long spell!'
Hindley named a fiddle, and then he asked Miss Cathy; she was hardly six
10   years old, but she could ride any horse in the stable, and she chose a whip.
He did not forget me; for he had a kind heart, though he was rather severe,
sometimes. He promised to bring me a pocketful of apples and pears, and then
he kissed his children good-bye, and set off.
It seemed a long while to us all – the three days of his absence – and often did
15   little Cathy ask when he would be home. Mrs Earnshaw expected him by
supper-time, on the third evening; and she put off the meal hour after hour;
there were no signs of his coming, however, and at last the children got tired of
running down to the gate to look – Then it grew dark, she would have had them
to bed, but they begged sadly to be allowed to stay up; and, just about eleven
20   o'clock, the door-latch was raised quietly and in stept the master. He threw
himself into a chair, laughing and groaning, and bid them all stand off, for he
was nearly killed – he would not have another such walk for the three kingdoms.
'And at the end of it to be flighted to death!' he said, opening his great coat,
which he held bundled up in his arms. 'See here, wife; I was never so beaten
25   with anything in my life; but you must e'en take it as a gift of God; though it's as
dark almost as if it came from the devil.'
We crowded round, and, over Miss Cathy's head, I had a peep at a dirty,
ragged, black-haired child; big enough both to walk and talk – indeed, its face
looked older than Catherine's – yet, when it was set on its feet, it only stared
30   round, and repeated over and over again some gibberish that nobody could
understand. I was frightened, and Mrs Earnshaw was ready to fling it out of
doors: she did fly up – asking how he could fashion to bring that gipsy brat into
the house, when they had their own bairns to feed, and fend for? What he meant
to do with it, and whether he were mad?
35   The master tried to explain the matter; but he was really half dead with
fatigue, and all that I could make out, amongst her scolding, was a tale of his
seeing it starving, and houseless, and as good as dumb in the streets of
Liverpool where he picked it up and inquired for its owner – Not a soul knew to
whom it belonged, he said, and his money and time, being both limited, he
40   thought it better to take it home with him, at once, than run into vain expenses
there; because he was determined he would not leave it as he found it.
Well, the conclusion was that my mistress grumbled herself calm; and Mr
Earnshaw told me to wash it, and give it clean things, and let it sleep with the
children.
45   Hindley and Cathy contented themselves with looking and listening till
peace was restored; then, both began searching their father's pockets for the
presents he had promised them. The former was a boy of fourteen, but when he

drew out what had been a fiddle, crushed to morsels in the greatcoat, he
blubbered aloud, and Cathy, when she learnt the master had lost her whip in
50 attending on the stranger, showed her humour by grinning and spitting at the
stupid little thing, earning for her pains a sound blow from her father to teach
her cleaner manners.

bonny (6): healthy-looking
stept (20): stepped (old spelling)
flighted (23): frightened
e'en (25): even
brat (32): child (a word used to show contempt)
bairns (33): children
blubbered (49): cried noisily

Understanding and Appreciating

1   What reason did Mr Earnshaw give for only being able to bring small
    presents?
2   What shows that the children were impatient for their father to return?
3   Why was Mr Earnshaw 'groaning' when he returned (line 21)?
4   In what way might the child be considered 'a gift of God' (line 25)?
5   Which parts of the description of the child and his arrival might support the
    opposite view that he 'came from the devil' (line 26)?
6   What reasons did Mrs Earnshaw have for not welcoming the child into the
    family?
7   Why had Mr Earnshaw decided to bring the child home?
8   What effect is created by the constant reference to the child as 'it'?

Summary Writing

In a short paragraph of 60–80 words, explain (in your own words) why Hindley
and Cathy had been looking forward to their father's return, why they were
disappointed, and how they reacted.

Vocabulary

'Peep' (line 27) means to 'look furtively, often through a narrow opening'.
Choose the suitable word from the list below to describe the ways of looking in
the following sentences (you may need to change the form of the word):

examine, gaze, glance, glare, glimpse, observe, peer, stare.

1 The husband was so angry that he _glare_ at his wife for several minutes.
2 The driver _peer_ through the fog, trying to find his way.
3 The lawyer _examine_ the document carefully to see if there were any ambiguities.
4 I think I just _glimpse_ her coming out of the theatre last night.
5 The teacher _glance_ at his watch when he thought the students weren't looking.
6 He's so much in love with her that he just _gaze_ at her photo for hours.
7 My mother always said that it was rude to _stare_ at strangers.
8 The private detective had spent a month _observe_ the movements of the suspect, and was now ready to make his report.

Phrasal Verbs (take)

Complete the following phrasal verbs, using one of the following words:

aback, after, back, in, on, out on, over, up.

1 The Earnshaw family were clearly taken _aback_ by the arrival of Heathcliff.
2 My boss is always trying to get me to take _on_ more responsibility.
3 Since his illness, John has taken _up_ golf.
4 Mary's daughter takes _after_ her so much that it's difficult to tell them apart.
5 The teacher quarrelled with his wife, and then took his annoyance _take out on_ his students.
6 The workers were worried in case their firm was taken _over_ by a foreign company.
7 That song by the Beatles takes me _back_ to my student days in the 1960s.
8 Don't be taken _in_ by his smart appearance; he's really a dangerous criminal.

Role-play (Pairwork)

Student A: you are Mrs Earnshaw. The children have now gone to bed. Tell your husband what you think of his idea of bringing the strange child home.
Student B: you are Mr Earnshaw. Try to explain to your wife that you felt sorry for the child, and that you feel you should help those less fortunate than yourself.

Composition

'Should adopted children have the right to know who their real parents are?'
Discuss. (About 350 words.)

Unit 3 LOVE

Vanity Fair
by William Makepeace Thackeray
(1847–48)

'Perhaps love is like the ocean,
Full of conflict, full of pain . . .'
  Perhaps Love by John Denver

'. . . love is not love
Which alters when it alteration finds'
  Sonnet by Shakespeare

Discussion

- What does being in love really mean?
- In what ways can love be 'full of conflict, full of pain'?
- Do you agree with Shakespeare that someone truly in love would not change their feelings even if there was a change in the other person's feelings?

The Novel

The story is set in the second decade of the nineteenth century, at the time of Napoleon and the Battle of Waterloo, and centres around the fortunes of two very different girls, Becky and Amelia. Becky is beautiful, adventurous and unprincipled and determined to get on in the world, whereas Amelia is quieter and virtuous. Major William Dobbin has long been in love with Amelia, to no avail, and, in this extract, he finally announces that he is giving up.

'Indeed it does, madam,' said the Major. 'If I have any authority in this house—'

'Authority, none!' broke out Amelia. 'Rebecca, you stay with me. *I* won't desert you because you have been persecuted, or insult you because – because
5 Major Dobbin chooses to do so. Come away, dear.' And the two women made towards the door.

William opened it. As they were going out, however, he took Amelia's hand, and said, 'Will you stay a moment and speak to me?'

'He wishes to speak to you away from me,' said Becky, looking like a martyr.
10 Amelia gripped her hand in reply.

'Upon my honour, it is not about you that I am going to speak,' Dobbin said. 'Come back, Amelia,' and she came. Dobbin bowed to Mrs Crawley, as he shut the door upon her. Amelia looked at him, leaning against the glass: her face and her lips were quite white.

15 'I was confused when I spoke just now,' the Major said, after a pause, 'and I misused the word authority.'

'You did,' said Amelia, with her teeth chattering.

'At least I have claims to be heard,' Dobbin continued.

'It is generous to remind me of our obligations to you,' the woman answered.
20 'The claims I mean are those left me by George's father,' William said.

'Yes, and you insulted his memory. You did yesterday. You know you did. And I will never forgive you. Never!' said Amelia. She shot out each little sentence in a tremor of anger and emotion.

'You don't mean that, Amelia?' William said sadly. 'You don't mean that
25 these words, uttered in a hurried moment, are to weigh against a whole life's devotion? I think that George's memory has not been injured by the way in which I have dealt with it, and if we are come to bandying reproaches, I at least merit none from his widow and the mother of his son. Reflect, afterwards when – when you are at leisure, and your conscience will withdraw this accusation. It
30 does even now.' Amelia held down her head.

'It is not that speech of yesterday,' he continued, 'which moves you. That is but the pretext, Amelia, or I have loved you and watched you for fifteen years in vain. Have I not learned in that time to read all your feelings, and look into your thoughts? I know what your heart is capable of: it can cling faithfully to a
35 recollection, and cherish a fancy; but it can't feel such an attachment as mine deserves to mate with, and such as I would have won from a woman more generous than you. No, you are not worthy of the love which I have devoted to you. I knew all along that the prize I had set my life on was not worth the winning; that I was a fool, with fond fancies, too, bartering away my all of truth
40 and ardour against your little feeble remnant of love. I will bargain no more: I withdraw. I find no fault with you. You are very good-natured, and have done your best; but you couldn't – you couldn't reach up to the height of the attachment which I bore you, and which a loftier soul than yours might have been proud to share. Goodbye, Amelia! I have watched your struggle. Let it
45 end. We are both weary of it.'

Amelia stood scared and silent as William thus suddenly broke the chain by which she held him, and declared his independence and superiority. He had

placed himself at her feet so long that the poor little woman had been
accustomed to trample upon him. She didn't wish to marry him, but she wished
50 to keep him. She wished to give him nothing, but that he should give her all. It is
a bargain not unfrequently levied in love.

William's sally had quite broken and cast her down. *Her* assault was long
since over and beaten back.

'Am I to understand then, – that you are going – away, – William?' she said.
55 He gave a sad laugh. 'I went once before,' he said, 'and came back after
twelve years. We were young, then, Amelia. Goodbye. I have spent enough of
my life at this play.'

Whilst they had been talking, the door into Mrs Osborne's room had opened
ever so little; indeed, Becky had kept a hold of the handle, and had turned it on
60 the instant when Dobbin quitted it; and she heard every word of the
conversation that had passed between these two. 'What a noble heart that man
has,' she thought, 'and how shamefully that woman plays with it!' She admired
Dobbin; she bore him no rancour for the part he had taken against her. It was
an open move in the game, and played fairly. 'Ah!' she thought, 'if I could have
65 had such a husband as that – a man with a heart and brains too! I would not
have minded his large feet;' and running into her room she absolutely
bethought herself of something and write him a note, beseeching him to stop for
a few days – not to think of going – and that she could serve him with A.

The parting was over. Once more poor William walked to the door and was
70 gone; and the little widow, the author of all this work, had her will, and had won
her victory, and was left to enjoy it as she best might. Let the ladies envy her
triumph.

bandying (27): exchanging   sally (52): an outburst

Understanding and Appreciating

1   What does Dobbin mean by his use of 'authority' (line 1)?
2   How does Dobbin subsequently tone that statement down?
3   What is meant by the phrase 'to weigh against a whole life's devotion' (lines
    25–26)?
4   Explain what William (Dobbin) means by 'the prize I had set my life on' (line
    38).
5   What criticism of Amelia is implied in the sentence, 'a loftier soul than yours
    might have been proud to share' (the attachment) (lines 43–44)?
6   What do lines 62–63 imply had previously taken place between William and
    Becky?
7   Explain in your own words what 'she could serve him with A' means (line
    68).
8   In lines 71–72 the writer states 'Let the ladies envy her triumph'. What is the
    tone of the sentence, and what does the writer mean by it?

Summary Writing

In a short paragraph of 60–80 words, summarise (in your own words) the basis
of Amelia and William's past relationship, and how William feels now, as
described in lines 46–57.

Vocabulary

Re-phrase each of the following sentences, using one of the introductory verbs from the list below. (You may need to change the form of the word.) The first one has been done for you as an example.

admire, appreciate, approve, cherish, devote, idolize, regard, respect.

1   Dobbin was so much in love with Amelia that he treated her as a goddess.
    Dobbin idolized Amelia
2   Lyn and Alistair consider themselves good friends, but they are not really in love.
3   Michael was really grateful for the help that Tom had given him.
4   The director decided that the proposal was a good idea.
5   A secretary cannot possibly have any esteem for a boss who comes to work in jeans and an old sweater.
6   In the marriage ceremony, Alan promised to look after Gillian for the rest of their lives.
7   Mr Jones thinks so highly of Rubens that he has covered his walls with copies of his paintings.
8   A religious person spends most of his/her life serving God.

Phrasal Verbs (give)

Complete the following phrasal verbs, using one of the following words:

away (× 2), in, off, out, rise to, up, way.

1   Dobbin finally gave _____ all hope of ever marrying Amelia.
2   The director was told that he would have to give _____ to a younger man, and was therefore forced to retire.
3   'That cheese is giving _____ a strange smell!'
4   Because the regiment's motto was 'no surrender', the soldiers refused to give _____, and were all killed defending their position.
5   The bride looked radiant as she was given _____ by her father.
6   It was given _____ on the radio this morning that income tax is being reduced.
7   Despite the torture, it took two days before Guy Fawkes would give _____ the names of his friends.
8   The fact that Michael and Jane often had lunch together gave _____ various rumours about them.

Role-play (Pairwork)

Student A: you are Dobbin. Explain to your best friend what has just happened, and that you are very depressed.
Student B: you are Dobbin's best friend. You are glad he has finally ended his relationship with Amelia. Try to cheer him up with suggestions for the future.

Composition

Write a story entitled 'Love at First Sight'. (About 350 words.)

Unit 4 SURPRISES

The Woman in White by Wilkie Collins (1860)

Discussion

- Surprises can sometimes be enjoyable and sometimes frightening; how would you feel in a situation similar to the surprise party in the photograph?
- What kind of surprises would you regard as unpleasant?
- Which adjectives (other than 'frightened') would you use to describe your feelings when surprised by the sudden appearance of a stranger on the path in front of you at night?

The Novel

Walter Hartwright is a young teacher of drawing who lives in London. Having just been offered a post with a family in the North of England, he is walking home from saying good-bye to his mother and sister when he has a most unexpected meeting with 'a woman in white'.

There, in the middle of the broad, bright high-road—there, as if it had that moment sprung out of the earth or dropped from the heaven—stood the figure of a solitary Woman, dressed from head to foot in white garments, her face bent in grave inquiry on mine, her hand pointing to the dark cloud over London, as I
5 faced her.

I was far too seriously startled by the suddenness with which this extraordinary apparition stood before me, in the dead of night and in that lonely place, to ask what she wanted. The strange woman spoke first.

"Is that the road to London?" she said.

10 I looked attentively at her, as she put that singular question to me. It was then nearly one o'clock. All I could discern distinctly by the moonlight was a colourless, youthful face, meagre and sharp to look at about the cheeks and chin; large, grave, wistfully attentive eyes; nervous, uncertain lips; and light hair of a pale, brownish-yellow hue. There was nothing wild, nothing immodest

15 in her manner: it was quiet and self-controlled, a little melancholy and a little touched by suspicion; not exactly the manner of a lady, and, at the same time, not the manner of a woman in the humblest rank of life. The voice, little as I had yet heard of it, had something curiously still and mechanical in its tones, and the utterance was remarkably rapid. She held a small bag in her hand: and her

20 dress—bonnet, shawl, and gown all of white—was, so far as I could guess, certainly not composed of very delicate or very expensive materials. Her figure was slight, and rather above the average height—her gait and actions free from the slightest approach to extravagance. This was all that I could observe of her in the dim light and under the perplexingly strange circumstances of our

25 meeting. What sort of a woman she was, and how she came to be out alone in the high-road, an hour after midnight, I altogether failed to guess. The one thing of which I felt certain was, that the grossest of mankind could not have misconstrued her motive in speaking, even at that suspiciously late hour and in that suspiciously lonely place.

30 "Did you hear me?" she said, still quietly and rapidly, and without the least fretfulness or impatience. "I asked if that was the way to London."

"Yes," I replied, "that is the way: it leads to St. John's Wood and the Regent's Park. You must excuse my not answering you before. I was rather startled by your sudden appearance in the road; and I am, even now, quite

35 unable to account for it."

"You don't suspect me of doing anything wrong, do you? I have done nothing wrong. I have met with an accident—I am very unfortunate in being here alone so late. Why do you suspect me of doing wrong?"

She spoke with unnecessary earnestness and agitation, and shrank back from

40 me several places. I did my best to reassure her.

"Pray don't suppose that I have any idea of suspecting you," I said, "or any other wish than to be of assistance to you, if I can. I only wondered at your appearance in the road, because it seemed to me to be empty the instant before I saw you."

45 She turned, and pointed back to a place at the junction of the road to London and the road to Hampstead, where there was a gap in the hedge.

"I heard you coming," she said, "and hid there to see what sort of man you

14

were, before I risked speaking. I doubted and feared about it till you passed;
and then I was obliged to steal after you, and touch you."

50   Steal after me and touch me? Why not call to me? Strange, to say the least of
it.

"May I trust you?" she asked. "You don't think the worse of me because I
have met with an accident?" She stopped in confusion; shifted her bag from one
hand to the other; and sighed bitterly.

55   The loneliness and helplessness of the woman touched me. The natural
impulse to assist her and to spare her got the better of the judgment, the
caution, the worldly tact, which an older, wiser, and colder man might have
summoned to help him in this strange emergency.

"You may trust me for any harmless purpose," I said. "If it troubles you to
60 explain your strange situation to me, don't think of returning to the subject
again. I have no right to ask you for any explanations. Tell me how I can help
you; and if I can, I will."

"You are very kind, and I am very, very thankful to have met you." The first
touch of womanly tenderness that I had heard from her trembled in her voice as
65 she said the words; but no tears glistened in those large, wistfully attentive eyes
of hers, which were still fixed on me. "I have only been in London once before,"
she went on, more and more rapidly, "and I know nothing about that side of it,
yonder. Can I get a fly, or a carriage of any kind? Is it too late? I don't know. If
you could show me where to get a fly—and if you will only promise not to
70 interfere with me, and to let me leave you, when and how I please—I have a
friend in London who will be glad to receive me—I want nothing else—will you
promise?"

gait (22): way of walking
steal after (49): to walk quietly or secretly
a fly (68): a one-horse carriage, available for hire

Understanding and Appreciating

1   Why didn't Walter speak to the woman at first?
2   Why does he regard the question about the road to London as 'singular' (line
     10)?
3   Explain what is meant by 'a little touched by suspicion' (lines 15–16).
4   What inference might be drawn from the materials of her dress (lines
     19–21)?
5   In what way can the woman's 'earnestness and agitation' be described as
     'unnecessary' (line 39)?
6   How had the woman managed to appear so quickly and unexpectedly?
7   What is indicated by the fact that she 'shifted her bag from one hand to the
     other' (lines 53–54)?
8   Which potential response did Walter ignore in this situation?

Summary Writing

In a short paragraph of 60–80 words, summarise (in your own words) what Walter finally says to the woman, and what she asks him to do, as described in lines 59–72.

Vocabulary

Match the words or phrases based on 'high' on the left with the correct definition on the right. For example: 'the high-road' (line 1) = the main road.

1	to be high and dry	a	intellectual
2	high and low	b	extremely lively
3	highbrow	c	everywhere
4	to highlight	d	to look flushed
5	high-life	e	living like an aristocrat
6	high-spirited	f	to make prominent
7	to be on one's high horse	g	to be stranded, literally or figuratively
8	to have a high colour	h	to behave arrogantly

Phrasal Verbs (come)

Match the phrasal verbs on the left with the correct definitions on the right.

1	to come about	a	to be of greater importance than something else
2	to come across		
3	to come before	b	to inherit
4	to come of	c	to meet by chance
5	to come into	d	to reveal a fact unexpectedly
6	to come out with	e	to regain consciousness
7	to come to	f	to happen
8	to come up to	g	to be equal to
		h	to result from

Role-play (Pairwork)

Student A: you are Walter Hartwright. Describe this strange meeting to a friend, and explain that you are puzzled.

Student B: you are Walter's friend. Ask for more details about the strange woman, and give your opinion as to how she came to be on the road.

Composition

Write a story entitled 'The Surprise', using the following opening sentences. (About 350 words.)

   Mr Chapman arrived home from work at 6.30 p.m., as he had done for the last 20 years. 'I'm back, dear', he called out, as he opened the front door, but this time there was no reply.

Unit 5 CHILDHOOD

Great Expectations by Charles Dickens (1860–61)

'The first thing I can remember is waking up in the night, crying and shaking because of a terrible dream. My mother came in and cuddled me until I fell back to sleep'.

'My earliest recollection is of going to the hospital to see my new baby brother. I took my favourite teddy bear with me; I suppose I thought he'd be able to play with it'

'I suppose I can't really remember much before my first day at school, when I got lost and was found crying in a corner of the changing room'.

Discussion

- Are any of these memories similar to your earliest ones? How far back can you remember?
- Can you remember anything that particularly frightened you as a child?

The Novel

After an introductory page, the novel opens in a churchyard on the Kent marshes

by the River Thames. Pip, an orphan who is looked after by his married sister, is standing looking at his family's tombstones, when he is suddenly approached by an escaped prisoner.

'Hold your noise!' cried a terrible voice, as a man started up from among the graves at the side of the church porch. 'Keep still, you little devil, or I'll cut your throat!'

A fearful man, all in coarse grey, with a great iron on his leg. A man with no
5 hat, and with broken shoes, and with an old rag tied round his head. A man who had been soaked in water, and smothered in mud, and lamed by stones, and cut by flints, and stung by nettles, and torn by briars; who limped, and shivered, and glared and growled; and whose teeth chattered in his head as he seized me by the chin.
10 'O! Don't cut my throat, sir,' I pleaded in terror. 'Pray don't do it, sir.'

'Tell us your name!' said the man. 'Quick!'

'Pip, sir.'

'Once more,' said the man, staring at me. 'Give it mouth!'

'Pip. Pip, sir.'
15 'Show us where you live,' said the man. 'Pint out the place!'

I pointed to where our village lay, on the flat in-shore among the alder-trees and pollards, a mile or more from the church.

The man, after looking at me for a moment, turned me upside down, and emptied my pockets. There was nothing in them but a piece of bread. When the
20 church came to itself – for he was so sudden and strong that he made it go head over heels before me, and I saw the steeple under my feet – when the church came to itself, I say, I was seated on a high tombstone, trembling, while he ate the bread ravenously.

'You young dog,' said the man, licking his lips, 'what fat cheeks you ha'
25 got.'

I believe they were fat, though I was at that time undersized for my years, and not strong.

'Darn Me if I couldn't eat em,' said the man, with a threatening shake of his head, 'and if I han't half a mind to't!'
30 I earnestly expressed my hope that he wouldn't, and held tighter to the tombstone on which he had put me; partly, to keep myself upon it; partly, to keep myself from crying.

'Now lookee here!' said the man. 'Where's your mother?'

'There, sir!' said I.
35 He started, made a short run, and stopped and looked over his shoulder.

'There, sir!' I timidly explained. 'Also Georgiana. That's my mother.'

'Oh!' said he, coming back. 'And is that your father alonger your mother?'

'Yes, sir,' said I; 'him too; late of this parish.'

'Ha!' he muttered then, considering. 'Who d'ye live with – supposin' you're
40 kindly let to live, which I han't made up my mind about?'

'My sister, sir – Mrs Joe Gargery – wife of Joe Gargery, the blacksmith, sir.'

'Blacksmith, eh?' said he. And looked down at his leg.

After darkly looking at his leg and me several times, he came closer to my tombstone, took me by both arms, and tilted me back as far as he could hold me;
45 so that his eyes looked most powerfully down into mine, and mine looked most helplessly up into his.

'Now lookee here,' he said, 'the question being whether you're to be let to live. You know what a file is?'

'Yes, sir.'
50 'And you know what wittles is?'

'Yes, sir.'

After each question he tilted me over a little more, so as to give me a greater sense of helplessness and danger.

'You get me a file.' He tilted me again. 'And you get me wittles.' He tilted me
55 again. 'You bring 'em both to me.' He tilted me again. 'Or I'll have your heart and liver out.' He tilted me again.

I was dreadfully frightened, and so giddy that I clung to him with both hands, and said, 'If you would kindly please to let me keep upright, sir, perhaps I shouldn't be sick, and perhaps I could attend more.'
60 He gave me a most tremendous dip and roll, so that the church jumped over its own weather-cock.

pint (15): point
alder-trees (16): a tree of the birch family, found especially in marshy ground
pollards (17): trees whose branches have been cut
Darn Me (28): Damn me (a form of swearing)
late (38): no longer alive
a file (48): a tool with small cutting edges (normally used for smoothing surfaces)
wittles (50): (victuals) food

Understanding and Appreciating

1 What do we learn about the prisoner's movements just before this scene, from the description in lines 5–9?
2 Why does the prisoner turn Pip upside down (line 18)?
3 What effect is achieved by Dickens's description of the church in lines 19–22, and 60–61?
4 How do the prisoner's words in lines 24–29 emphasise the fact that he is ravenous?
5 Why is the prisoner startled by Pip's reply, 'There, Sir!' (line 34)?
6 What is implied in the prisoner's words, 'Blacksmith, eh?' (line 42)?
7 What exactly was the advantage the prisoner gained by tilting Pip back (line 44)?
8 Explain why Pip speaks lines 58–59 in the way that he does.

Summary Writing

In a short paragraph of 60–80 words, explain how all these factors combine to create a frightening effect on Pip; the place, the prisoner himself, and what the prisoner says and does.

Vocabulary

Lame (see line 6) means 'to be unable to walk properly due to injury or disability'. Match the following words, which indicate different ways of walking, with the correct definition on the right.

1	creep	a	to walk or climb over rough or steep ground
2	limp	b	to walk forward, (nearly) tripping over something
3	scramble	c	to struggle through water
4	slip	d	to walk in a leisurely manner
5	stagger	e	to lose your balance, often on a greasy or icy surface
6	stroll	f	to walk unsteadily, swaying from side to side
7	stumble	g	to walk in a secretive way, possibly to avoid detection
8	wade	h	to walk with difficulty, because of a bad leg

Idioms

Match the idioms, based on parts of the body, on the left with the correct definition on the right.

1	to pull someone's leg	a	to cease having anything to do with the matter
2	to give your right arm for something	b	to reach a crisis
3	to wash your hands of something	c	to settle down in a new situation
4	to put your finger on something	d	to have a joke at someone else's expense
5	to come to a head	e	to be overcharged
6	to lose face	f	to mention the exact point (of a problem)
7	to pay through the nose	g	to want something very much
8	to find your feet	h	to suffer shame or humiliation

Role-play (Pairwork)

You are a mother and father who need a regular babysitter two evenings a week to look after your children, aged two and five. What qualities would you look for in a babysitter, and how old should he/she be? Decide with your partner what kind of person would be suitable.

Composition

'Childhood is the happiest period of your life.' Discuss. (About 350 words.)

Unit 6 WEALTH

Silas Marner by George Eliot (1861)

Discussion

- What would you do if you lost a great deal of money, as in the stock market crash of 1987?
- Would losing a great deal of money affect someone's personality in any way?
- What sort of things might compensate someone for financial loss in life?

The Novel

Silas Marner was forced to leave his circle of friends in Lantern Yard (in a northern town) when he was falsely accused of stealing money. He settled down in the village of Raveloe as a weaver, but his only interest was in hoarding the gold coins he earned. His world was shattered one night when they were stolen.

Some time later, while Silas is having a kind of fit in which he loses consciousness, a small baby crawls into his cottage and lies down by the fire. (Her mother, Molly, a working-class woman, has just died in the snow outside, on her way to expose the fact that she is secretly married to the local squire's eldest son, Godfrey Cass.)

This morning he had been told by some of his neighbours that it was New
Year's Eve, and that he must sit up and hear the old year rung out and the new
rung in, because that was good luck, and might bring his money back again.
This was only a friendly Raveloe-way of jesting with the half-crazy oddities of a
5   miser, but it had perhaps helped to throw Silas into a more than usually excited
state. Since the on-coming of twilight he had opened his door again and again,
though only to shut it immediately at seeing all distance veiled by the falling
snow. But the last time he opened it the snow had ceased, and the clouds were
parting here and there. He stood and listened, and gazed for a long
10   while—there was really something on the road coming towards him then, but
he caught no sign of it; and the stillness and the wide trackless snow seemed to
narrow his solitude, and touched his yearning with the chill of despair. He went
in again, and put his right hand on the latch of the door to close it—but he did
not close it: he was arrested, as he had been already since his loss, by the
15   invisible wand of catalepsy, and stood like a graven image, with wide but
sightless eyes, holding open his door, powerless to resist either the good or evil
that might enter there.

When Marner's sensibility returned, he continued the action which had
been arrested, and closed his door, unaware of the chasm in his consciousness,
20   unaware of any intermediate change, except that the light had grown dim, and
that he was chilled and faint. He thought he had been too long standing at the
door and looking out. Turning towards the hearth, where the two logs had
fallen apart, and sent forth only a red uncertain glimmer, he seated himself on
his fireside chair, and was stooping to push his logs together, when, to his
25   blurred vision, it seemed as if there were gold on the floor in front of the hearth.
Gold!—his own gold—brought back to him as mysteriously as it had been
taken away! He felt his heart begin to beat violently, and for a few moments he
was unable to stretch out his hand and grasp the restored treasure. The heap of

gold seemed to glow and get larger beneath his agitated gaze. He leaned
30 forward at last, and stretched forth his hand; but instead of the hard coin with
the familiar resisting outline, his fingers encountered soft warm curls. In utter
amazement, Silas fell on his knees and bent his head low to examine the marvel:
it was a sleeping child—a round, fair thing, with soft yellow rings all over its
head. Could this be his little sister come back to him in a dream—his little sister
35 whom he had carried about in his arms for a year before she died, when he was a
small boy without shoes or stockings? That was the first thought that darted
across Silas's blank wonderment. *Was* it a dream? He rose to his feet again,
pushed his logs together, and, throwing on some dried leaves and sticks, raised
a flame; but the flame did not disperse the vision—it only lit up more distinctly
40 the little round form of the child and its shabby clothing. It was very much like
his little sister. Silas sank into his chair powerless, under the double presence of
an inexplicable surprise and a hurrying influx of memories. How and when had
the child come in without his knowledge? He had never been beyond the door.
But along with that question, and almost thrusting it away, there was a vision of
45 the old home and the old streets leading to Lantern Yard—and within that
vision another, of the thoughts which had been present with him in those far-off
scenes. The thoughts were strange to him now, like old friendships impossible
to revive; and yet he had a dreamy feeling that this child was somehow a
message come to him from that far-off life: it stirred fibres that had never been
50 moved in Raveloe—old quiverings of tenderness—old impressions of awe at the
presentiment of some Power presiding over his life; for his imagination had not
yet extricated itself from the sense of mystery in the child's sudden presence,
and had formed no conjectures of ordinary natural means by which the event
could have been brought about.

jesting (4): joking
wand (15): a rod used by magicians (used figuratively here)
catalepsy (15): a disease causing periods of unconsciousness
graven image (15): a statue or carved image used as an idol

Understanding and Appreciating

1   Why was Silas in a 'more than usually excited state' on New Year's Eve (line 5)?
2   What effect does the 'stillness and the wide, trackless snow' have on Silas (line 11)?
3   Explain what is meant by 'unaware of the chasm in his consciousness' (line 19)?
4   Why did Silas feel 'his heart begin to beat violently' (line 27)?
5   Which words are contrasted with 'hard coin' (line 30)?
6   What was Silas's purpose when he 'raised a flame' in the fire (lines 38–39)?
7   Which words in the text show that softer emotions have been aroused in Silas (lines 47–51)?
8   What has his imagination caused him to be unable to comprehend (lines 51–54)?

Summary Writing

In a short paragraph of 60–80 words, summarise (in your own words) what is said about Silas's sister in lines 34–41, and which feelings were revived in him, as described in lines 49–51.

Vocabulary

'Sensibility' in line 18 means 'capacity to feel' and it refers to Silas's return to consciousness. With a partner, write sentences to bring out the meaning of the following words or phrases based on the word 'sense':

(a) senseless   (b) sensible   (c) sensitive   (d) sensational   (e) a sixth sense
(f) to come to your senses

Idioms

Match the sentences, containing the idioms based on the word 'gold', on the left with the correct definitions on the right.

1	The children were as good as gold while you were away	a	to receive a large sum of money
2	The old lady has a heart of gold	b	a wonderful chance
3	His boss told him that going to America was a golden opportunity	c	something that makes a lot of money
4	The shop on the corner is a real goldmine	d	don't be deceived by appearances
5	My father was made redundant but the firm gave him a golden handshake	e	to behave perfectly
6	'All that glisters is not gold' (*The Merchant of Venice*) ('glister' = 'glitter')	f	to be very kind

Role-play (Pairwork)

Student A: you are a stockbroker who has lost a great deal of money in the recent financial crash. Try to 'break the news' to your husband/wife.
Student B: you are the stockbroker's husband/wife. You have got used to your prosperous way of life. React to your husband's/wife's news, and ask about the future.

Composition

The desire for money is the strongest factor that motivates human behaviour. Discuss. (About 350 words.)

Unit 7 MISUNDERSTANDINGS

The Return of the Native
by Thomas Hardy
(1878)

Discussion

- Look at the photograph and decide what kind of misunderstanding has occurred.
- What kind of misunderstandings might occur between the following people:
  boyfriend/girlfriend
  father/son, or mother/daughter
  teacher/student
  boss/secretary
- If you had unintentionally caused a misunderstanding of that kind, what would you do next?

The Novel

Clym Yeobright has returned from Paris to his native village and married Eustacia Vye, against the wishes of his mother. Eustacia had formerly been in love with Mr Wildeve, who has now married Clym's cousin, Thomasin. Mrs Yeobright has sent some money to Clym and to Thomasin, which, due to a chain of circumstances, fell into Mr Wildeve's hands at one stage. In this extract, Mrs Yeobright has come to ask Eustacia if Mr Wildeve has handed over to Clym the money that is rightfully his.

When Mrs. Yeobright approached, Eustacia surveyed her with the calm stare of a stranger.

The mother-in-law was the first to speak. 'I was coming to see you,' she said.

'Indeed!' said Eustacia with surprise, for Mrs. Yeobright, much to the girl's
5　mortification, had refused to be present at the wedding. 'I did not at all expect you.'

'I was coming on business only,' said the visitor, more coldly than at first. 'Will you excuse my asking this—Have you received a gift from Thomasin's husband?'

10　'A gift?'

'I mean money!'

'What—I myself?'

'Well, I meant yourself, privately—though I was not going to put it in that way.'

15　'Money from Mr. Wildeve? No—never! Madam, what do you mean by that?' Eustacia fired up all too quickly, for her own consciousness of the old attachment between herself and Wildeve led her to jump to the conclusion that Mrs. Yeobright also knew of it, and might have come to accuse her of receiving dishonourable presents from him now.

20　'I simply ask the question,' said Mrs. Yeobright. 'I have been——'

'You ought to have better opinions of me—I feared you were against me from the first!' exclaimed Eustacia.

'No. I was simply for Clym,' replied Mrs. Yeobright, with too much emphasis in her earnestness. 'It is the instinct of every one to look after their
25　own.'

'How can you imply that he required guarding against me?' cried Eustacia, passionate tears in her eyes. 'I have not injured him by marrying him! What sin have I done that you should think so ill of me? You had no right to speak against me to him when I have never wronged you.'

30　'I only did what was fair under the circumstances,' said Mrs. Yeobright more softly. 'I would rather not have gone into this question at present, but you compel me. I am not ashamed to tell you the honest truth. I was firmly convinced that he ought not to marry you—therefore I tried to dissuade him by all the means in my power. But it is done now, and I have no idea of
35　complaining any more. I am ready to welcome you.'

'Ah, yes, it is very well to see things in that business point of view,' murmured Eustacia with a smothered fire of feeling. 'But why should you think there is anything between me and Mr. Wildeve? I have a spirit as well as you. I am indignant; and so would any woman be. It was a condescension in me to be
40　Clym's wife, and not a manœuvre, let me remind you; and therefore I will not be treated as a schemer whom it becomes necessary to bear with because she has crept into the family.'

'Oh!' said Mrs. Yeobright, vainly endeavouring to control her anger. 'I have never heard anything to show that my son's lineage is not as good as the
45　Vyes'—perhaps better. It is amusing to hear you talk of condescension.'

'It was condescension, nevertheless,' said Eustacia vehemently. 'And if I had known then what I know now, that I should be living in this wild heath a month after my marriage, I—I should have thought twice before agreeing.'

50 'It would be better not to say that; it might not sound truthful. I am not aware that any deception was used on his part—I know there was not—whatever might have been the case on the other side.'

'This is too exasperating!' answered the younger woman huskily, her face crimsoning, and her eyes darting light. 'How can you dare to speak to me like that? I insist upon repeating to you that had I known that my life would from 55 my marriage up to this time have been as it is, I should have said *No*. I don't complain. I have never uttered a sound of such a thing to him; but it is true. I hope therefore that in the future you will be silent on my eagerness. If you injure me now you injure yourself.'

'Injure you? Do you think I am an evil-disposed person?'

60 'You injured me before my marriage, and you have now suspected me of secretly favouring another man for money!'

'I could not help what I thought. But I have never spoken of you outside my house.'

'You spoke of me within it, to Clym, and you could not do worse.'

65 'I did my duty.'

'And I'll do mine.'

'A part of which will possibly be to set him against his mother. It is always so. But why should I not bear it as others have borne it before me!'

'I understand you,' said Eustacia, breathless with emotion. 'You think me 70 capable of every bad thing. Who can be worse than a wife who encourages a lover, and poisons her husband's mind against his relative? Yet that is now the character given to me. Will you not come and drag him out of my hands?'

Mrs. Yeobright gave back heat for heat.

'Don't rage at me, madam! It ill becomes your beauty, and I am not worth 75 the injury you may do it on my account, I assure you. I am only a poor old woman who has lost a son.'

lineage (44): ancestry, the families from which he is descended
heath (47): an area of flat land, sometimes covered with small plants but with very few trees

Understanding and Appreciating

1   Why had Eustacia not expected Mrs Yeobright to visit her?
2   What does Mrs Yeobright mean when she says 'I was simply for Clym' (line 23)?
3   What does 'it' refer to in line 34?
4   What does Eustacia mean by her use of the word 'condescension' in line 45?
5   What has made Eustacia regret her marriage (lines 46–48)?
6   Explain what Mrs Yeobright means by 'whatever might have been the case on the other side' (line 51).
7   What is indicated by the description of Eustacia's face as 'crimsoning' (line 53)?
8   To what is Eustacia referring when she uses the word 'eagerness' in line 57?

Summary Writing

In a short paragraph of 60–80 words, explain (in your own words) why Eustacia misunderstands Mrs Yeobright's question about the money, and why it makes her so angry. (Take your information from lines 8–19 and 60–72.)

Vocabulary

Put the following lists of words expressing affection, anger and surprise into an order of intensity. Put 1 for the least intense, and 3 for the most intense.

Affection	Anger	Surprise
a) attracted by	a) furious	a) thunderstruck
b) devoted to	b) displeased	b) amazed
c) attached to	c) indignant	c) surprised

Idioms

In line 17 of the text, the expression 'to jump to a conclusion' is used (meaning: to come to a conclusion quickly and often incorrectly). In this exercise, match the idioms based on 'jump' on the left with the correct definition on the right.

1	to be jumpy	a	to do something before the expected time
2	to jump to it	b	to take an opportunity eagerly
3	to jump at the chance	c	not to wait your turn in a line
4	to jump the gun	d	to be nervous
5	to jump on someone	e	to do something straightaway
6	to jump the queue	f	to speak to someone as soon as he/she arrives

Role-play (Pairwork)

Student A: you live near a young man/woman who sometimes looks after your children. You have arranged for him/her to come over tonight (Tuesday) while you go to the theatre. Since the person has not arrived, you phone up to see if anything is wrong.

Student B: you are the young man/woman. You are getting ready to go to your best friend's birthday party tonight, as *you* had understood the arrangement to look after your neighbour's children was for *Thursday*. The telephone rings and it is your neighbour. Explain the misunderstanding and try to find a satisfactory solution.

Composition

Describe a family quarrel, caused by a misunderstanding. (About 350 words.)

Unit 8 SPACE

The First Men in the Moon
by H. G. Wells
(1901)

Discussion

- What adjectives could you use to describe people's reactions on July 21st 1969?
- Has this event had any effect on our lives in the last twenty years?
- When do you think space travel will be an everyday occurrence? In what other ways will life be different from today?

The Novel

Cavor, a scientist, invents a spaceship referred to as 'the sphere', and persuades his new friend, Bedford, to accompany him. On the moon, they are captured by moon creatures called Selenites, but manage to escape. They separate in an attempt to find their spaceship, which Bedford eventually does. Believing Cavor to have been killed, Bedford returns to Earth alone. After some time, to his great surprise, he is informed that telegraphic messages have been received from the moon. They have been sent by Cavor, and give a rather one-sided account of what took place.

Throughout, Cavor speaks of me as a man who is dead, but with a curious change of temper as he approaches our landing on the moon. "Poor Bedford," he says of me, and "this poor young man"; and he blames himself for inducing a young man, "by no means well equipped for such adventures," to leave a planet
5   "on which he was indisputably fitted to succeed" on so precarious a mission. I think he underrates the part my energy and practical capacity played in bringing about the realisation of his theoretical sphere. "We arrived," he says, with no more account of our passage through space than if we had made a journey of common occurrence in a railway train.
10   And then he becomes increasingly unfair to me. Unfair, indeed, to an extent I should not have expected in a man trained in the search for truth. Looking back over my previously written account of these things, I must insist that I have been altogether juster to Cavor than he has been to me. I have extenuated little and suppressed nothing. But his account is:—
15   "It speedily became apparent that the entire strangeness of our circumstances and surroundings—great loss of weight, attenuated but highly oxygenated air, consequent exaggeration of the results of muscular effort, rapid development of weird plants from obscure spores, lurid sky—was exciting my companion unduly. On the moon his character seemed to deteriorate. He
20   became impulsive, rash, and quarrelsome. In a little while his folly in devouring some gigantic vesicles and his consequent intoxication led to our capture by the Selenites—before we had had the slightest opportunity of properly observing their ways. . . ."

    (He says, you observe, nothing of his own concession to these same
25   "vesicles.")

    And he goes on from that point to say that "We came to a difficult passage with them, and Bedford mistaking certain gestures of theirs"—pretty gestures they were!—"gave way to a panic violence. He ran amuck, killed three, and perforce I had to flee with him after the outrage. Subsequently we fought with a
30   number who endeavoured to bar our way, and slew seven or eight more. It says much for the tolerance of these beings that on my recapture I was not instantly slain. We made our way to the exterior and separated in the crater of our arrival, to increase our chances of recovering our sphere. But presently I came upon a body of Selenites, led by two who were curiously different, even in form,
35   from any of these we had seen hitherto, with larger heads and smaller bodies, and much more elaborately wrapped about. And after evading them for some

time I fell into a crevasse, cut my head rather badly, and displaced my patella, and, finding crawling very painful, decided to surrender—if they would still permit me to do so. This they did, and, perceiving my helpless condition,
40 carried me with them again into the moon. And of Bedford I have heard or seen nothing more, nor, so far as I can gather, has any Selenite. Either the night overtook him in the crater, or else, which is more probable, he found the sphere, and, desiring to steal a march upon me, made off with it—only, I fear, to find it uncontrollable, and to meet a more lingering fate in outer space.''

extenuated (13): excused
attenuated (16): reduced in force, rarefied
vesicles (21): In this case it refers to a type of plant that can be eaten
ran amuck (28): ran about in a violent uncontrolled way
patella (37): knee-cap

Understanding and Appreciating

1   Why does Cavor describe Bedford as 'poor' in lines 2 and 3?
2   What did Cavor think he had deprived Bedford of by taking him to the moon?
3   What part did Bedford think he had played in helping to produce the sphere?
4   How would you describe Cavor's account of their arrival on the moon?
5   What effect, according to Cavor, did the environment on the moon have on Bedford?
6   Explain in your own words what the 'folly' was in eating the 'vesicles' (lines 20–23).
7   What does Cavor say about the Selenites character when he has been taken prisoner once again?
8   What reason does Cavor think Bedford must have had to take off in the sphere without him?

Summary Writing

In a short paragraph of 60–80 words, describe (in your own words) Bedford and Cavor's escape from the Selenites, and Cavor's subsequent recapture (lines 26–40).

Vocabulary

Match the words on the left (which are taken from lines 1–4 of the text) with the words nearest in meaning on the right.

1	to induce	a	dependent on chance
2	indisputable	b	fair
3	precarious	c	to deduce, discover
4	to underrate	d	excessively
5	just	e	to persuade
6	unduly	f	to attempt
7	to endeavour	g	something that cannot be argued with
8	to gather	h	to have too low an opinion of someone

Idioms

Match these idioms based on stars and the planets with the correct definitions:

1	to be over the moon	a	to try really hard
2	to be starry-eyed	b	to be ecstatically happy
3	to move heaven and earth	c	to have a high opinion of someone
4	to come down in the world	d	to be over-idealistic
5	to think the world of someone	e	to have an unofficial, second job
6	once in a blue moon	f	to lose social status
7	in a world of his/her own	g	to be totally absorbed in something
8	to moonlight	h	rarely

Role-play (Pairwork)

Student A: you have a rather risky plan for spending three years hitch-hiking around the world, and want your friend to come with you.

Student B: try to dissuade your friend from going on this venture, which you feel could be difficult and rather dangerous.

Composition

'It is difficult to justify expenditure on space research when a large part of the world is starving.' Discuss. (About 350 words.)

Unit 9 TRAVEL

A Room with a View by E. M. Forster
(1908)

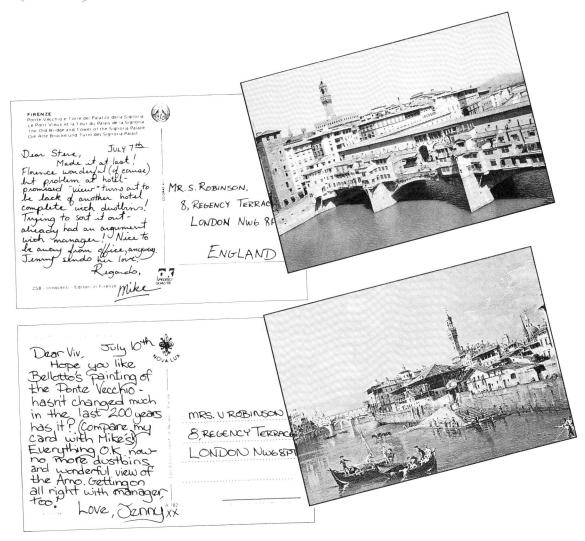

Discussion

- In what ways must life in Florence have changed since the eighteenth century?
- What do you think Mike said to the hotel manager about his room?
- Have you had any holidays where things went wrong? How were the problems dealt with?

The Novel

The story opens in a hotel in Florence, where various English tourists are staying. Lucy Honeychurch, a young English girl, has just arrived at the hotel, accompanied by Miss Bartlett, who is a less prosperous relative acting as a chaperone. On arriving at the hotel, there is a disappointment concerning their rooms.

'THE Signora had no business to do it,' said Miss Bartlett, 'no business at all. She promised us south rooms with a view close together, instead of which here are north rooms, here are north rooms, looking into a courtyard, and a long way apart. Oh, Lucy!'

5 'And a Cockney, besides!' said Lucy, who had been further saddened by the Signora's unexpected accent. 'It might be London.' She looked at the two rows of English people who were sitting at the table; at the row of white bottles of water and red bottles of wine that ran between the English people; at the portraits of the late Queen and the late Poet Laureate that hung behind the
10 English people, heavily framed; at the notice of the English church (Rev. Cuthbert Eager, M.A., Oxon), that was the only other decoration of the wall. 'Charlotte, don't you feel too, that we might be in London? I can hardly believe that all kinds of other things are just outside. I suppose it is one's being so tired.'

'This meat has surely been used for soup,' said Miss Bartlett, laying down
15 her fork.

'I wanted so to see the Arno. The rooms the Signora promised us in her letter would have looked over the Arno. The Signora had no business to do it at all. Oh, it is a shame!'

'Any nook does for me,' Miss Bartlett continued; 'but it does seem hard that
20 you shouldn't have a view.'

Lucy felt that she had been selfish. 'Charlotte, you mustn't spoil me: of course, you must look over the Arno, too. I meant that. The first vacant room in the front – '

'You must have it,' said Miss Bartlett, part of whose travelling expenses were
25 paid by Lucy's mother – a piece of generosity to which she made many a tactful allusion.

'No, no. You must have it.'

'I insist on it. Your mother would never forgive me, Lucy.'

'She would never forgive *me*.'

30 The ladies' voices grew animated, and – if the sad truth be owned – a little peevish. They were tired, and under the guise of unselfishness they wrangled. Some of their neighbours interchanged glances, and one of them – one of the ill-bred people whom one does meet abroad – leant forward over the table and actually intruded into their argument. He said:

35 'I have a view, I have a view.'

Miss Bartlett was startled. Generally at a pension people looked them over for a day or two before speaking, and often did not find out that they would 'do' till they had gone. She knew that the intruder was ill-bred, even before she glanced at him. He was an old man, of heavy build, with a fair, shaven face and

40 large eyes. There was something childish in those eyes, though it was not the childishness of senility. What exactly it was Miss Bartlett did not stop to consider, for her glance passed on to his clothes. These did not attract her. He was probably trying to become acquainted with them before they got into the swim. So she assumed a dazed expression when he spoke to her, and then said:

45 'A view? Oh, a view! How delightful a view is!'

'This is my son,' said the old man; 'his name's George. He has a view, too.'

'Ah,' said Miss Bartlett, repressing Lucy, who was about to speak.

'What I mean,' he continued, 'is that you can have our rooms, and we'll have yours. We'll change.'

50 The better class of tourist was shocked at this, and sympathized with the new-comers. Miss Bartlett, in reply, opened her mouth as little as possible, and said:

'Thank you very much indeed: that is out of the question.'

'Why?' said the old man, with both fists on the table.

55 'Because it is quite out of the question, thank you.'

Poet Laureate (9): the poet commissioned by the monarch to write poems on important occasions
nook (19): a small, quiet corner or place
peevish (31): irritable

Understanding and Appreciating

1 What is it that the Signora had 'no business to do' (line 1)?
2 What does Lucy mean when she says, 'we might be in London' (line 12)?
3 What is it that makes Miss Bartlett say, 'you must have it' in line 27 (referring to the first vacant room with a view)?
4 Why is it so startling when the old man says 'I have a view, I have a view' (line 35)?
5 What reasons does Miss Barlett have for considering the old man 'ill-bred' (line 38)?
6 What is meant by the expression 'before they got into the swim' (lines 43–44)?
7 What is Miss Bartlett's purpose in assuming a 'dazed expression' (line 44)?
8 Why did 'the better class of tourist ... sympathize with the new-comers' (lines 50–51)?

Summary Writing

In a short paragraph of 70–80 words, explain (in your own words) the problem about the rooms allocated to Miss Bartlett and Lucy, and why the old man's offer is not accepted.

Vocabulary

Match the words on the left (which have been taken from lines 1–41 of the text) with the words nearest in meaning on the right.

1	to spoil	a	indirect reference
2	tactful	b	old age
3	allusion	c	pretence
4	animated	d	to argue
5	guise	e	saying the right thing
6	to wrangle	f	to thrust oneself into something uninvited
7	to intrude	g	to over-indulge
8	senility	h	lively

Phrasal Verbs (get)

Match the sentence containing a phrasal verb with the correct definition on the right.

1	Alice always gets away with her bad behaviour.	a	to grow old
2	Keith really must get down to some hard work.	b	to avoid something unpleasant
3	My grandfather's getting on a bit now, I'm afraid.	c	to escape criticism or punishment
4	Mike and Jenny had an argument with the hotel manager when they first arrived, but they're getting on all right with him now.	d	to begin to concentrate on something
5	The teacher told the students to get on with their project work.	e	to recover
6	Richard always gets out of difficult jobs.	f	to be connected to someone on the telephone
7	Mr Brown was deeply in love with his wife, and never got over it when she died so unexpectedly at the age of thirty-five.	g	to continue
8	I tried to get through to you yesterday, but the line was engaged.	h	to have a friendly relationship with someone

Role-play (Pairwork)

Student A: you are the manager of a hotel, used to dealing with difficult customers. A new hotel guest comes up to you.

Student B: tell the manager about your room. It's small, dirty, overlooks the busy main road, and has no bath or toilet. This is not what you asked for when you booked.

Composition

Describe a holiday you have had when things did not go according to plan. (About 350 words.)

Unit 10 ACHIEVEMENT

Sons and Lovers by D. H. Lawrence (1913)

Match the famous people on the left with the correct achievement on the right.

1 Hippocrates (460–370 BC)
2 Ferdinand de Lesseps (1805–1894)
3 Leo Tolstoy (1828–1910)
4 Sigmund Freud (1856–1939)
5 Robert Baden Powell (1857–1941)

a Austrian psychiatrist, founder of psychoanalysis.
b English general, founder of the boy scouts.
c Greek physician, considered to be 'the father of medicine'.
d Russian novelist, author of *War and Peace*, sometimes regarded as the greatest novel ever written.
e French engineer, builder of the Suez Canal.

Discussion

- Which of these achievements would you regard as the greatest, and why?
- What do you regard as your greatest achievement when you were at school? How did your parents react?

The Novel

The story concerns the Morel family; Mr Morel is a rough, uneducated miner who is despised by his wife, whose background was more refined and who had been considered intellectual. Their son, Paul takes after his mother and is close to her; he, too, despises the rough ways of his father. In this extract, he has sent one of his paintings to a local exhibition, and just learns that it has won first prize.

One morning the postman came just as he was washing in the scullery. Suddenly he heard a wild noise from his mother. Rushing into the kitchen, he found her standing on the hearthrug wildly waving a letter and crying 'Hurrah!' as if she had gone mad. He was shocked and frightened.

5 'Why, mother!' he exclaimed.

She flew to him, flung her arms round him for a moment, then waved the letter crying:

'Hurrah, my boy! I knew we should do it!'

He was afraid of her – the small, severe woman with greying hair suddenly
10 bursting out in such frenzy. The postman came running back, afraid something had happened. They saw his tipped cap over the short curtain. Mrs Morel rushed to the door.

'His picture's got first prize, Fred,' she cried, 'and is sold for twenty guineas.'

'My word, that's something like!' said the young postman, whom they had
15 known all his life.

'And Major Moreton has bought it!' she cried.

'It looks like meanin' something, that does, Mrs Morel, said the postman, his blue eyes bright. He was glad to have brought such a lucky letter. Mrs Morel went indoors and sat down, trembling. Paul was afraid lest she might have
20 misread the letter, and might be disappointed after all. He scrutinized it once, twice. Yes, he became convinced it was true. Then he sat down, his heart beating with joy.

'Mother!' he exclaimed.

'Didn't I *say* we should do it!' she said, pretending she was not crying.
25 He took the kettle off the fire and mashed the tea.

'You didn't think, mother – –' he began tentatively.

'No, my son – not so much – but I expected a good deal.'

'But not so much,' he said.

'No – no – but I knew we should do it.'
30 And then she recovered her composure, apparently at least. He sat with his shirt turned back, showing his young throat almost like a girl's, and the towel in his hand, his hair sticking up wet.

'Twenty guineas, mother! That's just what you wanted to buy Arthur out. Now you needn't borrow any. It'll just do.'
35 'Indeed, I shan't take it all,' she said.

'But why?'

'Because I shan't.'

'Well – you have twelve pounds, I'll have nine.'

They cavilled about sharing the twenty guineas. She wanted to take only the
40 five pounds she needed. He would not hear of it. So they got over the stress of emotion by quarrelling.

Morel came home at night from the pit, saying:

'They tell me Paul's got first prize for his picture, and sold it to Lord Henry Bentley for fifty pound.'
45 'Oh, what stories people do tell!' she cried.

'Ha!' he answered. 'I said I wor sure it wor a lie. But they said tha'd told Fred Hodgkisson.'

'As if I would tell him such stuff!'

'Ha!' assented the miner.

50 But he was disappointed nevertheless.

'It's true he has got the first prize,' said Mrs Morel.

The miner sat heavily in his chair.

'Has he, beguy!' he exclaimed.

He stared across the room fixedly.

55 'But as for fifty pounds – such nonsense!' She was silent awhile. 'Major Moreton bought it for twenty guineas, that's true.'

'Twenty guineas! Tha niver says!' exclaimed Morel.

'Yes, and it was worth it.'

'Ay!' he said. 'I don't misdoubt it. But twenty guineas for a bit of a paintin' as
60 he knocked off in an hour or two!'

He was silent with conceit of his son. Mrs Morel sniffed, as if it were nothing.

'And when does he handle th' money?' asked the collier.

'That I couldn't tell you. When the picture is sent home, I suppose.'

There was silence. Morel stared at the sugar-basin instead of eating his
65 dinner. His black arm, with the hand all gnarled with work, lay on the table. His wife pretended not to see him rub the back of his hand across his eyes, nor the smear in the coal-dust on his black face.

scullery (1): a small room next to the kitchen, often used for washing dishes
guineas (13): a guinea was one pound and one shilling (=£1.05)
wor (46): was (dialect)
tha'd (46): you had (dialect)
beguy (53): By God! (dialect: a form of swearing, used here to express surprise)
Tha niver (57): You never (dialect, also used here to express surprise)

Understanding and Appreciating

1 What causes Paul to be 'shocked and frightened' (line 4)?
2 What is implied by Mrs Morrel's use of 'we' in lines 8, 24, and 29?
3 Explain what the postman means when he says, 'My word, that's something like!' (line 14).
4 Explain in your own words why Paul 'scrutinized' the letter twice (lines 20–21).
5 What is the underlying cause of the disagreement about the amount of money Paul should give to his mother (lines 33–40)?
6 What was Mr Morrel 'disappointed' about (line 50)?
7 What is implied in Mr Morrel's remark, 'twenty guineas for a bit of a paintin' as he knocked off in an hour or two!' (lines 59–60)?
8 How does the writer suggest that Mrs Morrel is ashamed of her husband and his occupation (lines 65–67)?

Summary Writing

In a short paragraph of 70–80 words, explain (in your own words) the difference between Mr and Mrs Morrel's reactions to Paul's prize.

Vocabulary

Put the following lists of words expressing fear, joy and sadness into an order of intensity. Put 1 for the least intense, and 3 for the most intense. (The first column comes from the text.)

Fear	Joy	Sadness
(a) to tremble with emotion	(a) to be delighted	(a) to be melancholic
(b) to be frightened	(b) to be ecstatic	(b) to be depressed
(c) to be in a frenzy	(c) to be pleased	(c) to feel unhappy

Phrasal Verbs (put)

Complete the following phrasal verbs, using one of the following words:

across, aside, down to, in for, off (× 2), out, up with.

1 Mrs Morel clearly had to put _____ her husband's lack of refinement.
2 Mrs Morel intends to put _____ some of the money in case it is needed to buy Arthur out of the army.
3 If a job involving painting were advertised, Paul would probably put _____ it.
4 Mr Morel was rather put _____ when he found out that Paul had not won fifty pounds.
5 Because Paul didn't expect his father to be interested, he might have put _____ telling him about the prize, but his father mentioned it first.
6 Mrs Morel put her husband's bad manners _____ his poor upbringing.
7 Because his father didn't understand him, Paul had difficulty in putting _____ his idea, and so he dropped the subject.
8 Paul might have wanted to become an artist, but was rather put _____ by his father's lack of interest and support.

Role-play (Pairwork)

Student A: you are Mrs Morel. You are thrilled by your son's achievement, and talk excitedly about it to your husband.

Student B: you are Mr Morel. You can't understand what all the fuss is about, and don't think it is right that a painting should be worth more than several weeks' wages from the coal mine. You wish your son had a real 'man's job'.

Composition

Write a story which ends as follows: 'So Michael had won the prize; he had attained his ambition, but at what cost to himself and his future life?' (About 350 words.)

Unit 11   MANIPULATION

1984 by George Orwell
(1949)

Discussion

- These two advertisements were placed in the national press by two opposing groups in the debate over smoking. How do they use language to get their point across?
- Do you think governments sometimes use emotive language in their campaigns against health problems, such as smoking or AIDS? Are there any inherent dangers in this kind of manipulation?

The Novel

1984 portrays a totalitarian state, where the government keeps an eye on everything you do. This is summed up in the famous line 'Big Brother is Watching You'. 'Newspeak', a new form of language, has been introduced whose purpose is explained at the start of the extract, which also explains the three types of vocabulary. ('Oldspeak' is the term used to describe the language before this and 'Ingsoc' means 'English Socialism', which in other words means 'the Party' or the state.)

The purpose of Newspeak was not only to provide a medium of expression for the world-view and mental habits proper to the devotees of Ingsoc, but to make all other modes of thought impossible. It was intended that when Newspeak had been adopted once and for all and Oldspeak forgotten, a heretical thought –
5 that is, a thought diverging from the principles of Ingsoc – should be literally unthinkable, at least so far as thought is dependent on words. Its vocabulary was so constructed as to give exact and often very subtle expression to every meaning that a Party member could properly wish to express, while excluding all other meanings and also the possibility of arriving at them by indirect
10 methods.

The A vocabulary. The A vocabulary consisted of the words needed for the business of everyday life – for such things as eating, drinking, working, putting on one's clothes, going up and down stairs, riding in vehicles, gardening, cooking, and the like. It was composed almost entirely of words that we already
15 possess – words like *hit, run, dog, tree, sugar, house, field* – but in comparison with the present-day English vocabulary their number was extremely small, while their meanings were far more rigidly defined. All ambiguities and shades of meaning had been purged out of them. So far as it could be achieved, a Newspeak word of this class was simply a staccato sound expressing *one* clearly
20 understood concept. It would have been quite impossible to use the A vocabulary for literary purposes or for political or philosophical discussion. It was intended only to express simple, purposive thoughts, usually involving concrete objects or physical actions.

The B vocabulary. The B vocabulary consisted of words which had been
25 deliberately constructed for political purposes: words, that is to say, which not only had in every case a political implication, but were intended to impose a desirable mental attitude upon the person using them. Without a full understanding of the principles of Ingsoc it was difficult to use these words correctly. In some cases they could be translated into Oldspeak, or even into
30 words taken from the A vocabulary, but this usually demanded a long paraphrase and always involved the loss of certain overtones. The B words were a sort of verbal shorthand, often packing whole ranges of ideas into a few syllables, and at the same time more accurate and forcible than ordinary language.
35 The B words were in all cases compound words. They consisted of two or more words, or portions of words, welded together in an easily pronounceable form. The resulting amalgam was always a noun-verb, and inflected according

to the ordinary rules. To take a single example: the word *goodthink*, meaning, very roughly, 'orthodoxy', or, if one chose to regard it as a verb, 'to think in an orthodox manner'. This inflected as follows: noun-verb, *goodthink*; past tense and past participle, *goodthinked*; present participle, *goodthinking*; adjective, *goodthinkful*; adverb, *goodthinkwise*; verbal noun, *goodthinker*.

The C vocabulary. The C vocabulary was supplementary to the others and consisted entirely of scientific and technical terms. These resembled the scientific terms in use to-day, and were constructed from the same roots, but the usual care was taken to define them rigidly and strip them of undesirable meanings. They followed the same grammatical rules as the words in the other two vocabularies. Very few of the C words had any currency either in everyday speech or in political speech. Any scientific worker or technician could find all the words he needed in the list devoted to his own speciality, but he seldom had more than a smattering of the words occurring in the other lists. Only a very few words were common to all lists, and there was no vocabulary expressing the function of Science as a habit of mind, or a method of thought, irrespective of its particular branches. There was, indeed, no word for 'Science', any meaning that it could possibly bear being already sufficiently covered by the word *Ingsoc*.

Understanding and Appreciating

1 Explain, in your own words, how Newspeak would make 'all other modes of thought impossible' (line 3).
2 What were the main two differences between the 'A vocabulary' and Standard English vocabulary?
3 Why was it not possible to use the 'A vocabulary' for 'philosophical discussion' (lines 20–21)?
4 What happened if words from the 'B vocabulary' were translated into 'Oldspeak'?
5 What is implied in the statement that 'goodthink' is 'to think in an orthodox manner'?
6 In what way is the 'C vocabulary' considered to be 'supplementary' (line 43)?
7 Explain what is meant by 'undesirable meanings' (lines 46–47).
8 What was the effect of the fact that scientists only had 'a smattering of the words occurring in the other lists' (line 51)?

Summary Writing

In a short paragraph of 70–80 words, summarise (in your own words) the main points of the 'A and B vocabulary'.

Role-play (Pairwork)

Student A: you are the chairman of the Tobacco Advisory Council. You feel that the government's campaign against smoking is unfair and undemocratic, and may also lead to unemployment in the tobacco industry. You are now meeting the Health Minister to put these points to him/her.

Student B: you are the Health Minister and have been asked to meet the chairman of the Tobacco Advisory Council. Listen to his/her points, but try to counter them, and explain that the government campaign will continue.

Vocabulary

Read the following report of the murder of the President of a distant country.

'The President was killed at 11.00 a.m. yesterday by two men wearing masks and carrying machine guns. They fired repeatedly until the President fell to the ground, and then made their escape using a stolen car'.

1   Do you think the writer was for or against the President, or neutral?
2   Put the following words into the correct columns to show whether you think they would be used in a press report by supporters of the government or the revolutionary army.

heroic glorious cowardly despicable freedom fighter terrorist
patriotic struggle step towards freedom evil campaign blow to democracy

Press Report (Government)	Press Release (Revolutionary Army)

Composition

Making use of some of the vocabulary in the exercise above, write two short press articles about the killing of the President (of about 150 words each), one from the government's point of view and the other from that of the revolutionary army. (You may need to add some further details of your own about the incident.)

Unit 12   CIVILIZATION

Lord of the Flies by William Golding *(1954)*

Discussion

- In 1620, the original settlers in America, the 'Pilgrim Fathers', signed an agreement to bind them all into one self-governing community. What matters do you think they had to consider in setting up a new community?
- What problems were likely to arise in the early years?
- What negative qualities in human nature might have become apparent?

The Novel

The story concerns a group of schoolboys who are isolated on a remote island (during a major war), and examines the way their civilized attitudes and behaviour gradually disintegrate into savage and basic instincts. In the extract, Jack and the choirboys, now known as the hunters, no longer accept the democratic assemblies, and the use of a large sea-shell called a 'conch' to allow freedom of speech. Jack tells his group to hold Ralph, the boy elected as leader, and his fat friend, known as Piggy and also the twins, Sam and Eric, known as 'Samneric' (since they are always together).

"I said 'grab them'!"

The painted group moved round Samneric nervously and unhandily. Once more the silvery laughter scattered.

Samneric protested out of the heart of civilization.

5 "Oh, I say!"

" – honestly!"

Their spears were taken from them.

"Tie them up!"

10 Ralph cried out hopelessly against the black and green mask.

"Jack!"

"Go on. Tie them."

Now the painted group felt the otherness of Samneric, felt the power in their own hands. They felled the twins clumsily and excitedly. Jack was inspired. He

15 knew that Ralph would attempt a rescue. He struck in a humming circle behind him and Ralph only just parried the blow. Beyond them the tribe and the twins were a loud and writhing heap. Piggy crouched again. Then the twins lay, astonished, and the tribe stood round them. Jack turned to Ralph and spoke between his teeth.

20 "See? They do what I want."

There was silence again. The twins lay, inexpertly tied up, and the tribe watched Ralph to see what he would do. He numbered them through his fringe, glimpsed the ineffectual smoke.

His temper broke. He screamed at Jack.

25 "You're a beast and a swine and a bloody, bloody thief!"

He charged.

Jack, knowing this was the crisis, charged too. They met with a jolt and bounced apart. Jack swung with his fist at Ralph and caught him on the ear. Ralph hit Jack in the stomach and made him grunt. Then they were facing each

30 other again, panting and furious, but unnerved by each other's ferocity. They became aware of the noise that was the background to this fight, the steady shrill cheering of the tribe behind them.

Piggy's voice penetrated to Ralph.

"Let me speak."

35 He was standing in the dust of the fight, and as the tribe saw his intention the shrill cheer changed to a steady booing.

Piggy held up the conch and the booing sagged a little, then came up again to strength.

"I got the conch!"

40 He shouted.

"I tell you, I got the conch!"

Surprisingly, there was silence now; the tribe were curious to hear what amusing thing he might have to say.

Silence and pause; but in the silence a curious air-noise, close by Ralph's

45 head. He gave it half his attention – and there it was again; a faint "Zup!" Someone was throwing stones: Roger was dropping them, his one hand still on the lever. Below him, Ralph was a shock of hair and Piggy a bag of fat.

"I got this to say. You're acting like a crowd of kids."

The booing rose and died again as Piggy lifted the white, magic shell.

50 "Which is better – to be a pack of painted niggers like you are, or to be sensible like Ralph is?"

A great clamour rose among the savages. Piggy shouted again.

"Which is better – to have rules and agree, or to hunt and kill?"

55 Again the clamour and again – "Zup!"

Ralph shouted against the noise.

"Which is better, law and rescue, or hunting and breaking things up?"

Now Jack was yelling too and Ralph could no longer make himself heard. Jack had backed right against the tribe and they were a solid mass of menace
60 that bristled with spears. The intention of a charge was forming among them; they were working up to it and the neck would be swept clear. Ralph stood facing them, a little to one side, his spear ready. By him stood Piggy still holding out the talisman, the fragile, shining beauty of the shell. The storm of sound beat at them, an incantation of hatred. High overhead, Roger, with a sense of
65 delirious abandonment, leaned all his weight on the lever.

Ralph heard the great rock long before he saw it. He was aware of a jolt in the earth that came to him through the soles of his feet, and the breaking sound of stones at the top of the cliff. Then the monstrous red thing bounded across the neck and he flung himself flat while the tribe shrieked.

70 The rock struck Piggy a glancing blow from chin to knee; the conch exploded into a thousand white fragments and ceased to exist. Piggy, saying nothing, with no time for even a grunt, travelled through the air sideways from the rock, turning over as he went. The rock bounded twice and was lost in the forest. Piggy fell forty feet and landed on his back across that square, red rock in the
75 sea. His head opened and stuff came out and turned red. Piggy's arms and legs twitched a bit, like a pig's after it has been killed. Then the sea breathed again in a long slow sigh, the water boiled white and pink over the rock; and when it went, sucking back again, the body of Piggy was gone.

niggers (50): negroes (an offensive term)
bristled with spears (60): contained a large number of spears sticking out
talisman (63): a lucky charm

Understanding and Appreciating

1 What is meant by the phrase 'out of the heart of civilization' (line 4)?
2 What is the effect of the constant description of Jack's boys as 'the painted group' or 'the tribe'?
3 What is implied by the fact that Jack 'spoke between his teeth' (lines 18–19)?
4 In what way is it a moment of crisis, when Ralph charges Jack (line 26)?
5 What causes the boys 'cheering' (line 32) to turn to 'booing' (line 36)?
6 Explain what is meant by 'a sense of delirious abandonment' (lines 64–65).
7 What is the symbolic implication of the breaking of the conch?
8 Which two parts of the description of Piggy's death compare it to that of a pig's (lines 70–78)?

Summary Writing

In a short paragraph of 60–80 words, summarise (in your own words) what Piggy tries to say in his appeal to the hunters, and explain why it is not successful.

Vocabulary

In the text, Jack's boys are described as 'a tribe'. For the sentences below, choose the suitable word from the following list of words describing different kinds of groups: band clan(s) class crowd(s) generation race society troop

1 In Scotland, there were often battles between the different _____.
2 The English are often described as a rather cold _____.
3 Robin Hood and his _____ of outlaws lived in Sherwood Forest.
4 The Prime Minister wants to do something about the trouble caused by large football _____.
5 The captain told his _____ that they were the worst soldiers he had ever seen.
6 'Do you think England still has a _____ system?' asked the American visitor.
7 Parents often misunderstand their children because they are from a different _____.
8 The Freemasons are a kind of secret _____ which still has a lot of influence in high places.

Phrasal Verbs (work)

Match the sentences containing a phrasal verb with the correct definition on the right.

1 The boys still hadn't attacked Ralph and Piggy, but they were working up to it.

2 I can't seem to work up any enthusiasm for this new project.

3 'Do you think you will be happy working under a foreign boss?' asked the interviewer.

4 John doesn't want to come to London, but I'm working on him.

5 'Were you able to work out question 10 in the Maths exam?' asked the teacher.

a to try to persuade someone
b to prepare to do something gradually
c to find the answer
d to be in an inferior position to someone at work
e to arouse feelings or interest

Role-play (Pairwork)

You are both co-directing a film of 'Lord of the Flies'. Discuss how you would film the scene leading up to and including the death of Piggy. Which aspects would you focus on and for how long, what use would you make of colour, would you have any background music, etc.?

Composition

'Man produces evil as a bee produces honey.' (William Golding.) Discuss. (About 350 words.)

Unit 13 AMBITION

Room at the Top by John Braine
(1957)

Martina Navratilova

Margaret Thatcher

Madonna

Maradona

Paul Getty

Harrison Ford

Discussion

- How 'ambitious' do you think these people had to be to get to the top?
- What do you think is involved in being 'ambitious'? What sort of sacrifices might have to be made?
- How determined would you be to achieve your own ambition? Would you marry to further your career, for example?

The Novel

The story is told in the first person, in a modern colloquial style by Joe Lampton, a working-class young man who is ruthless in his determination to 'get to the top'. He meets Susan Brown, the daughter of a successful self-made businessman, and eventually marries her and takes a highly-paid job in her father's company. In this extract, it is early on in their relationship and they have arranged to meet outside the local theatre.

SUSAN was already there when I reached the Grand. Against the black buildings of Leddersford her face was fresh and glowing.

'Hello darling.' I took both her hands. 'Sorry I'm late.'

'You're very naughty.' She squeezed my hands. 'I won't go out with you
5 again.' She held out her face for a kiss. 'I've been longing for that. Aren't I wicked?'

'You're the joy of my life,' I said, feeling for a moment very old. I took the evening paper from my pocket. 'There's a good film at the Odeon. Or a mediocre play at the Grand. Or what do you fancy?'
10 She looked at her feet. 'Don't be angry with me. But I don't want to go to the pictures. Or the theatre.'

'Of course I'm not angry. But if we're going for a walk, you'll have to tell me where. I'm a stranger here.'

'Ooh,' she said. 'Wicked, wicked. I never said I wanted to go for a walk.
15 There's Benton Woods though. I've a friend up there. But we needn't see her.'

She took my arm, holding it tightly as we walked over to the Benton bus stop. Passing the warehouses with their heavy, oily but curiously non-industrial smell of raw wool and the cramped littered offices with their mahogany furniture and high stools and the Gothic Wool Exchange straight out of Doré I
20 felt as the owners of the big cars outside, the gaffers, masters, overlords, must feel: the city was mine, a loving mother, its darkness and dirtiness was the foundation of my big house in Ilkley or Harrogate or Burley, my holiday at Biarritz or Monte Carlo, my suit from my own personal roll of cloth: Susan took all the envy out of me at that very moment, she made me rich. We walked
25 slowly, looking in all the shop windows; I bought a pair of made-to-measure aniline calf brogues, a made-to-measure shirt in real silk, a dozen wool ties, a fur felt trilby at five guineas, a beaver shaving-brush, and a Triumph roadster. I bought Susan a big flask of Coty, a mink cape, a silver hairbrush, a nylon negligee, and a jar of crystallized ginger. Or I would have done if the shops
30 hadn't all for some unaccountable reason been closed.

The bus had wooden seats; they reminded her of travelling third-class on the Continent. She chattered in her high, clear voice about Rouen and Paris and Versailles and Rheims and St Malo and Dinan and Montmartre and Montparnasse and the Louvre and the Comédie Française – but I never had
35 the feeling she was showing off, she hadn't a trace of self-consciousness; she'd been to all these places, they'd interested her very much, and she wanted to tell me all about them. Leddersford is a place where they don't like people who put on airs. To speak Standard English is in itself suspect; they call it talking

well-off. And to talk about holidays abroad is one of the almost infallible marks
40 of the stuck-up, the high-and-mighty, who are no better than they should be.
All the people on the top deck had been listening to Susan; but there were no
signs of resentment on their faces. Instead there was that pleased indulgent
look, that wistful admiration (the princess has come amongst us, close enough
for us to touch her if we dared) that I was to become accustomed to everywhere
45 I took her. I've often thought that if I wanted to put paid to Communism once
and for all, I'd have a hundred girls like Susan ride on buses the length and
breadth of Great Britain.

Doré (19): Paul Gustave Doré (1833–83), a French artist famous for his paintings
of biblical scenes
aniline calf brogues (26): strong, outdoor shoes
a fur felt trilby (26–27): a soft hat with a dent along the top and a narrow brim
a Triumph roadster (27): a sports car with no roof
a big flask of Coty (28): a large bottle of perfume

Understanding and Appreciating

1   How does the writer emphasize the fact that Susan is 'fresh and glowing'
    (line 2)?
2   How does the reader know that Susan does not mean it when she says, 'I
    won't go out with you again' (lines 4–5)?
3   How could you guess the meaning of 'the pictures' in line 11?
4   What does Susan feel is implied in the idea of going for a walk (line 12)?
5   What is it that makes Joe feel 'the city was mine' (line 21)?
6   How could you guess the meaning of 'gaffers' in line 20?
7   What is the purpose of the sentence beginning 'Or I would have done if...'
    (lines 29–30)?
8   What effect is achieved by the repetition of 'and' in lines 32–34?

Summary Writing

In a short paragraph of 70–80 words, explain (in your own words) why talking
about foreign holidays would *normally* cause resentment, and why it does *not*
do so in this case (lines 31–47).

Vocabulary 1

Which of the following qualities do you think a prospective employer would regard as positive, negative, or neutral, if they were used in a reference for a job? (You might not agree on some qualities!)

determined   ruthless   ambitious   persistent   selfish
energetic   reliable   sensitive   precise

Positive	Negative	Neutral

Vocabulary 2

Chatter (see line 32) means 'to talk quickly or incessantly'. Choose the suitable word from the list below to describe different ways of talking in the following sentences (you may need to change the form of the words):

address, babble, debate, discuss, gossip, have a word, have words, lecture.

1   Women are often unfairly accused of _____ over the garden fence.
2   The boss was annoyed; 'I want to _____ with you', he said.
3   The visiting speaker _____ the meeting for more than an hour.
4   'Shall we _____ this matter at our next meeting?' the director suggested.
5   Students often _____ motions such as 'This house believes that smoking causes serious damage to health'.
6   'What on earth was that drunken driver _____ about?' said the policeman. 'I couldn't understand a word he said.'
7   'Oh, hello, have you got a minute?' said the boss. 'I'd like to _____ with you.'
8   Professor Smith normally _____ twice a week, and spends the rest of his time on academic research.

Role-play (Pairwork)

Student A: you are Joe Lampton. Speak to Susan's father, Mr Brown, and try to persuade him to let you marry her.
Student B: you are Mr Brown. You don't think Joe is good enough for your daughter. Offer to give him some money if he agrees to leave the district.

Composition

Which would you rather do, have a job in a big city which might lead to a top position, or work in a quiet village in the country with no prospects of promotion? (About 350 words.)

Unit 14 INTERPRETATIONS

The Jewel in the Crown by Paul Scott (1966)

The Fighting Temeraire (1838) by J. M. W. Turner (1775–1851)

Discussion

- The Temeraire was an old warship which had taken part in the Battle of Trafalgar in 1805. By 1838 she was old-fashioned and was taken up the Thames to be broken up. This painting is often thought to be a symbolic one; if so, what is Turner trying to say, and how does he achieve his effect?
- Do you know of any other famous paintings that have a special significance or symbolic interpretation?

The Novel

The story is set in India in 1942, during the Second World War and five years before India's independence. In the novel, Scott explores British and Indian attitudes and feelings, especially in the character of Hari Kumar, who is an Indian with an English upbringing, and who is falsely accused of attacking an English girl, Daphne Manners. The opening of the novel centres around another character, Miss Crane, who is an elderly, unmarried lady who teaches at the mission school intended to educate local children in the Christian religion. Miss Crane, having stood up to some rioters who attempted to enter the school, has reluctantly become a kind of heroine, and has decided to ask her superior, Mr Cleghorn, for a transfer to another school. On leaving, she is given a painting which has a special meaning for her.

When Mr. Cleghorn returned from leave, anxious for news of what he had only heard as rumour, she decided to apply for a transfer so that she could get on with her job without constant reminders of what she thought of as her false position. She told Mr. Cleghorn that it was quite impossible to teach children
5 who, facing her, saw her as a cardboard heroine and no doubt had, each of them, only one eye on the blackboard because the other was fixed on the doorway, expectant of some further disturbance they wanted her to quell. Mr. Cleghorn said that he would be sorry to see her go, but that he quite understood and that if she really meant what she said he would write personally to mission
10 headquarters to explain matters.

When the instructions for her transfer came she discovered that she had been promoted by being put in sole charge of the school at Ranpur. Before she left there was a tea, and then the presentation of the picture – a larger, more handsomely framed copy of the picture on the wall behind her desk in the
15 Muzzafirabad schoolroom, a semi-historical, semi-allegorical picture entitled *The Jewel in Her Crown*, which showed the old Queen (whose image the children now no doubt confused with the person of Miss Crane) surrounded by representative figures of her Indian Empire: Princes, landowners, merchants, money-lenders, sepoys, farmers, servants, children, mothers, and remarkably
20 clean and tidy beggars. The Queen was sitting on a golden throne, under a crimson canopy, attended by her temporal and spiritual aides: soldiers, statesmen and clergy. The canopied throne was apparently in the open air because there were palm trees and a sky showing a radiant sun bursting out of bulgy clouds such as, in India, heralded the wet monsoon. Above the clouds
25 flew the prayerful figures of the angels who were the benevolent spectators of the scene below. Among the statesmen who stood behind the throne one was painted in the likeness of Mr. Disraeli holding up a parchment map of India to which he pointed with obvious pride but tactful humility. An Indian prince, attended by native servants, was approaching the throne bearing a velvet
30 cushion on which he offered a large and sparkling gem. The children in the school thought that this gem was the jewel referred to in the title. Miss Crane had been bound to explain that the gem was simply representative of tribute, and that the jewel of the title was India herself, which had been transferred from the rule of the British East India Company to the rule of the British crown in
35 1858, the year after the Mutiny when the sepoys in the service of the Company (that first set foot in India in the seventeenth century) had risen in rebellion, and attempts had been made to declare an old moghul prince king in Delhi, and that the picture had been painted after 1877, the year in which Victoria was persuaded by Mr. Disraeli to adopt the title Empress of India.
40 *The Jewel in Her Crown* was a picture about which Miss Crane had very mixed feelings. The copy that already hung on the classroom wall in Muzzafirabad when she first went there as assistant to Mr. Cleghorn she found useful when teaching the English language to a class of Muslim and Hindu children. This is the Queen. That is her crown. The sky there is blue. Here there are clouds in the
45 sky. The uniform of the sahib is scarlet. Mr. Cleghorn, an ordained member of the Church and an enthusiastic amateur scholar of archaeology and anthropology, and much concerned with the impending, never-got-down-to

composition of a monograph on local topography and social customs, had
devoted most of his time to work for the Church and for the older boys in the
50   middle school. He did this at the expense of the junior school, as he was aware.
When Miss Crane was sent to him from Lahore in response to his requests for
more permanent help in that field of his responsibility he had been fascinated to
notice the practical use she made of a picture which, to him, had never been
more than something hanging on the wall to brighten things up.
55   He was fond of remarking on it, whenever he found her in class with half a
dozen wide-eyed children gathered round her, looking from her to the picture as
she took them through its various aspects, step by step. "Ah, the picture again,
Miss Crane," he would say, "admirable, admirable. I should never have
thought of it. To teach English and at the same time love of the English."
60   She knew what he meant by love of the English. He meant love of their
justice, love of their benevolence, love – anyway – of their good intentions. As
often as she was irritated by his simplicity, she was touched by it. He was a good
man: tireless, inquisitive, charitable. Mohammedanism and Hinduism, which
still frightened her in their outward manifestations, merely amused him: as a
65   grown man might be amused by the grim, colourful but harmless games of
children. If there were times when she thought him heedless of the misery of
men, she could not help knowing that in his own way he never forgot the glory of
God. Mr. Cleghorn's view was that God was best served, best glorified, by the
training and exercise of the intellect.

sepoys (35): Indian soldiers under British discipline
moghul (37): an Indian emperor
sahib (45): a form of address used by Indians to European men (used here to
mean an English officer')

Understanding and Appreciating

1   Explain, in your own words, why Miss Crane felt it 'impossible to teach' in
her present position (line 4).
2   What was the surprising result of Miss Crane's application for a transfer?
3   What is implied in the description of the beggars in the painting as
'remarkably clean and tidy' (lines 19–20)?
4   What is 'tactful' about the humility displayed by Mr Disraeli while pointing to
the map of India in the painting (line 28)?
5   What practical use had Miss Crane made of the other copy of the painting?
6   Explain the phrase 'at the expense of', as used in line 50.
7   What is implied in the difference between 'benevolence' and 'good
intentions' in line 61?
8   In what way might Mr Cleghorn have been 'heedless of the misery of men'
(lines 66–67)?

Summary Writing

In a short paragraph of 60–80 words, explain (in your own words) how the
painting is both 'semi-historical' and 'semi-allegorical' (lines 15–39).

Vocabulary

Match the words on the left (which have been taken from the text) with the words nearest in meaning on the right.

1	leave	a	concerned with life, and not the spirit
2	to quell	b	appearance
2	sole	c	permission to go on holiday
4	to herald	d	something of value paid to a superior power
5	temporal	e	suppress, stop happening
6	tribute	f	paying no attention to
7	manifestation	g	announce the arrival of
8	heedless	h	exclusive

Idioms

Match the idioms, based on 'paint' and 'picture', on the left with the correct definitions on the right.

1	to be as pretty as a picture	a	to be very content
2	to put someone in the picture	b	to describe something
3	to picture something	c	to look beautiful
4	to be a picture of happiness	d	to have a lively celebration
5	to paint a picture of something	e	to imagine
6	to paint the town red	f	to give information

Role-play (Pairwork)

Student A: you are presenting a farewell gift to a colleague who is retiring from your company. Say why the staff will miss him/her and wish him/her luck in the future.

Student B: you are the person who is retiring. After receiving your farewell present, make a short speech of thanks, mentioning why you've enjoyed working for this company and stating plans for the future.

Composition

Describe a day in your life when something really important happened to you. (About 350 words.)

Unit 15   SECLUSION

Hotel du Lac by Anita Brookner
(1984)

Discussion

- Which adjectives would you use to describe the scene?
- What kind of a holiday could you have in an area like this? What kind of person would most enjoy it?
- If you wanted to 'get away from it all', where would you go?

The Novel

The story is set in a lake-side hotel in Switzerland, and concerns a woman called Edith Hope. Gradually it becomes apparent that she has left England for a while to get over the embarrassment of not arriving at the church for her own wedding, when she was due to marry a rather dull man called Geoffrey. She has been involved in a close relationship with David, whom she loves dearly, but who is already married. This extract describes the Hotel du Lac.

The Hotel du Lac (Famille Huber) was a stolid and dignified building, a house of repute, a traditional establishment, used to welcoming the prudent, the well-to-do, the retired, the self-effacing, the respected patrons of an earlier era of tourism. It had made little effort to smarten itself up for the passing trade
5 which it had always despised. Its furnishings, although austere, were of excellent quality, its linen spotless, its service impeccable. Its reputation among knowledgeable professionals attracted apprentices of good character who had a serious interest in the hotel trade, but this was the only concession it made to a recognition of its own resources. As far as guests were concerned, it took a
10 perverse pride in its very absence of attractions, so that any visitor mildly looking for a room would be puzzled and deflected by the sparseness of the terrace, the muted hush of the lobby, the absence of piped music, public telephones, advertisements for scenic guided tours, or notice boards directing one to the amenities of the town. There was no sauna, no hairdresser, and
15 certainly no glass cases displaying items of jewellery; the bar was small and dark, and its austerity did not encourage people to linger. It was implied that prolonged drinking, whether for purposes of business or as a personal indulgence, was not *comme il faut*, and if thought absolutely necessary should be conducted either in the privacy of one's suite or in the more popular
20 establishments where such leanings were not unknown. Chambermaids were rarely encountered after ten o'clock in the morning, by which time all household noises had to be silenced; no vacuuming was heard, no carts of dirty linen were glimpsed, after that time. A discreet rustle announced the reappearance of the maids to turn down the beds and tidy the rooms once the
25 guests had finished changing to go down to dinner. The only publicity from which the hotel could not distance itself was the word of mouth recommendations of patrons of long standing.

What it had to offer was a mild form of sanctuary, an assurance of privacy, and the protection and the discretion that attach themselves to blamelessness.
30 This last quality being less than attractive to a surprising number of people, the Hotel du Lac was usually half empty, and at this time of the year, at the end of the season, was resigned to catering for a mere handful of guests before closing its doors for the winter. The few visitors who were left from the modest number who had taken their decorous holiday in the high summer months were,
35 however, treated with the same courtesy and deference as if they were treasured patrons of long standing, which, in some cases, they were. Naturally, no attempt was made to entertain them. Their needs were provided for and their characters perused with equal care. It was assumed that they would live up to the hotel's standards, just as the hotel would live up to theirs. And if any
40 problems were encountered, those problems would be dealt with discreetly. In this way the hotel was known as a place which was unlikely to attract unfavourable attention, a place guaranteed to provide a restorative sojourn for those whom life had mistreated or merely fatigued. Its name and situation figured in the card indexes of those whose business it is to know such things.
45 Certain doctors knew it, many solicitors knew it, brokers and accountants knew it. Travel agents did not know it, or had forgotten it. Those families who benefit from the periodic absence of one of their more troublesome members treasured

it. And the word got round.

And of course it was an excellent hotel. And its situation on the lake was
50 agreeable. The climate was not brilliant, but in comparison with other, similar,
resorts, it was equable. The resources of the little town were not extensive, but
cars could be hired, excursions could be taken, and the walking was pleasant if
unexciting. The scenery, the view, the mountain, were curiously unemphatic,
as if delineated in the watercolours of an earlier period. While the young of all
55 nations hurtled off to the sun and the beaches, jamming the roads and the
airports, the Hotel du Lac took a quiet pride, and sometimes it was very quiet
indeed, in its isolation from the herd, knowing that it had a place in the memory
of its old friends, knowing too that it would never refuse a reasonable request
from a new client, provided that the new client had the sort of unwritten
60 references required from an hotel of this distinction, and that the request had
come from someone whose name was already on the Huber family's files, most
of which went back to the beginning of the century.

comme il faut (18): correct behaviour (a French expression used in English)
decorous (34): in good taste

Understanding and Appreciating

1 What do you understand by the phrase 'an earlier era of tourism' (lines 3–4)?
2 How did the hotel manage to attract good staff (lines 6–9)?
3 Why do you think the hotel takes a 'perverse pride in its very absence of
   attractions' (line 10)?
4 How does the hotel manage to attract new clients (lines 25–27)?
5 In what circumstances might someone require 'a mild form of sanctuary'
   (line 28)?
6 Explain what is meant by 'It was assumed that they would live up to the
   hotel's standards, just as the hotel would live up to theirs' (lines 38–39).
7 Why do you think the hotel 'figured in the card indexes' of certain people
   (line 44)?
8 What is implied in the use of 'herd' (line 57)?

Summary Writing

In a short paragraph of 60–80 words, summarise (in your own words) what life
was like in the hotel, as described in lines 9–25.

Vocabulary 1

Match the words on the left (which have been taken from lines 1–35 of the text) with the words nearest in meaning on the right.

1	traditional	a	good manners
2	prudent	b	perfect
3	austere	c	a confident assertion
4	impeccable	d	cautious
5	indulgence	e	respect
6	assurance	f	customary
7	courtesy	g	plain, not decorated
8	deference	h	giving way to one's desire for pleasure

Vocabulary 2

There are certain foreign expressions used in English, such as *comme il faut* in line 18 of the text. In this exercise, match the expression on the left with the correct definition on the right.

1	*bona fide*	a	I've found it!
2	*carte blanche*	b	a way of working
3	*coup d'etat*	c	knowing the right way to do things
4	*de rigeur*	d	per head (= per person)
5	*eureka*	e	obligatory
6	*modus operandi*	f	to be given a free hand
7	*per capita*	g	genuine, sincere
8	*savoir-faire*	h	a violent overthrow of the government

Role-play (Pairwork)

Student A: you are recovering from an operation, and staying at the Hotel du Lac. You speak enthusiastically about the hotel to a fellow guest after dinner.

Student B: you are a guest at the Hotel du Lac. You find everything incredibly boring, and wish you had gone somewhere else. Disagree politely with your fellow guest's remarks.

Composition

Last year you had a wonderful holiday in Florence, staying in a pension like the one mentioned in *A Room With A View*. This year you are at the Hotel du Lac, and find it very boring and disappointing compared to last year's holiday. Write to your best friend, showing why you feel like this. (About 300 words.)

ANSWER KEY

Unit 1 *Emma*

Understanding and Appreciating

1   It was because her mother had died when Emma was young, and her sister had left home to get married.
2   It refers to Emma and Miss Taylor.
3   It is because it is clear that the relationship between Emma and Miss Taylor was more like that of sisters, and that Miss Taylor did not attempt to exercise her authority.
4   She was allowed to do whatever she wanted, and tended to think too highly of herself.
5   The words 'sorrow', 'loss', 'grief' and 'mournful' are more usually applied to a funeral than a marriage.
6   There is absolutely nothing to find fault with; he would therefore be a trustworthy, reliable and honourable man.
7   They had been able to have a closer relationship once Emma's sister had left home.
8   Clearly, Emma will not be able to enjoy such a close relationship with Miss Taylor, even though she is only half a mile away, since she will be a married woman with other responsibilities.

Summary

When Emma was young, Miss Taylor not only taught her and played with her, but also looked after her when she was ill. Once Emma's sister had left home, Miss Taylor was able to devote all her attention to Emma. She was clearly a most unselfish friend, doing whatever she could to help Emma and joining in whatever activities Emma suggested, and loving her too much to notice any faults in Emma's character. (73 words)

Vocabulary

Positive	Negative	Neutral
affectionate	sarcastic	indulgent*
generous	vindictive	self-effacing*
gentle		sensitive*
sympathetic		

*It depends on how you interpret them!

Idioms

1 g   2 e   3 h   4 f   5 a   6 d   7 c   8 b

Unit 2 *Wuthering Heights*

Understanding and Appreciating

1   He was going on foot, and it was a long way.
2   They keep running down to the gate to look for him, and ask to stay up late.
3   It was because he had walked a long way carrying the child.
4   He could be considered a 'gift of God' as he has arrived suddenly and unexpectedly totally 'out of the blue'.
5   They are the parts where the child is described as 'dirty' and 'black-haired' and as speaking in a way that cannot be understood.
6   It is difficult enough for her to keep her own family fed and clothed without taking in an outsider.
7   The child was all alone, and Mr Earnshaw did not have either the time or the money to investigate matters in Liverpool.
8   The use of 'it' creates a sub-human effect and helps to give the impression that the child is wild and different from the other children.

Summary

Hindley and Cathy had been looking forward to their father's return because he had promised to bring them back a present each. When Hindley found that his fiddle had been crushed, he burst into tears. Cathy's whip had been lost when her father was looking after the child, so she took her anger out on Heathcliff by spitting at him.
(60 words)

Vocabulary

1 glared   2 peered   3 examined   4 glimpsed   5 glanced   6 gazes   7 stare   8 observing

Phrasal Verbs (take)

1 aback   2 on   3 up   4 after   5 out on   6 over   7 back   8 in

Unit 3 *Vanity Fair*

Understanding and Appreciating

1   Dobbin is assuming that his special relationship with Amelia gives him certain privileges in her house.
2   He has to admit that he was wrong to use the word 'authority' since he does not have any real authority in Amelia's house.
3   Dobbin means that his long period of affection for Amelia ought to allow him to be excused for making a small mistake.
4   He means marrying Amelia.
5   He is implying that she has been too proud to marry him, although other, worthier women might have been pleased to.
6   It implies that there has been some previous argument or discussion in which Dobbin has spoken against her.
7   It means she could help him to win Amelia's love.
8   The tone is ironic; the writer implies that Amelia's apparent victory is a hollow one, since she has lost Dobbin and will be alone.

Summary

Dobbin has idolized Amelia and spent years being a loving and devoted friend, gaining little in return. Amelia had shown no desire to marry him, but had not wanted to lose his devoted friendship either. Finally Dobbin sees the light and realises that he has been wasting his time and that Amelia has not been worthy of his love. He therefore decides to leave.
(64 words)

Vocabulary

1   Dobbin idolized Amelia.
2   Lyn and Alistair regard themselves as good friends.
3   Michael (really) appreciated Tom's help.
4   The director approved of the idea.
5   A secretary cannot respect a boss who . . .
6   Alan promised to cherish Gillian.
7   Mr Jones admires Reubens so much that . . .
8   A religious person devotes most of his/her life to serving God.

Phrasal Verbs (give)

1 up   2 way   3 off   4 in   5 away   6 out   7 away   8 rise to

Unit 4 *The Woman in White*

Understanding and Appreciating

1   He was so surprised by her sudden appearance.
2   He did not expect a woman to be walking to London at that time of night.

3   Previous experience has caused her to be suspicious of strangers.
4   As they were not of an expensive kind, it might be inferred that she is not an upper-class lady.
5   She did not need to be worried, since Walter does not suspect her of any wrongdoing, and only wants to help her.
6   She had hidden behind a gap in the hedge, and only came out when she saw what kind of man he was.
7   It shows that she is worried and nervous, and not sure what to do.
8   He ignored any feelings of being careful and of considering the matter in any more detail, and followed his natural feeling of wanting to help.

Summary

Walter tells the woman that he will help her in anything which is not harmful and that she does not need to explain the details of her situation. The woman explains that she does not really know London, and asks him to show her where she could get a carriage to visit her friend there. She asks him to promise to let her go as and when she wants, without interference.
(71 words)

Vocabulary

1 g   2 c   3 a   4 f   5 e   6 b   7 h   8 d

Phrasal Verbs (come)

1 f   2 c   3 a   4 h   5 b   6 d   7 e   8 g

Unit 5 *Great Expectations*

Understanding and Appreciating

1   He had obviously been running across the country to escape capture, and had been outdoors for some time.
2   He wants to see if there is anything in Pip's pocket.
3   It shows the situation from the child's point of view.
4   He is so hungry that he could almost eat Pip.
5   He thinks Pip's mother is still alive, and just behind them.
6   He realises that a blacksmith would be able to get the 'great iron' off his leg.
7   It allowed him to look down directly into Pip's eyes, and therefore made his words more threatening and frightening.
8   Pip speaks in a very polite manner in order not to offend the prisoner and cause him to keep his promise of cutting his throat.

Summary

The effect of being alone in a churchyard, looking on to lonely marshes, is emphasised by the sudden appearance of the prisoner. He looks wild and desperate, due to his time on the run; his clothes are wet, muddy and torn, and his teeth chatter from the cold. He speaks to Pip in an abrupt, threatening manner, and treats him very roughly, alternately turning him upside down and tilting him backwards.
(71 words)

Vocabulary

1 g   2 h   3 a   4 e   5 f   6 d   7 b   8 c

Idioms

1 d   2 g   3 a   4 f   5 b   6 h   7 e   8 c

Unit 6 *Silas Marner*

Understanding and Appreciating

1   It was because he had been told that sitting up to see the New Year in, might bring his money back.
2   It made him feel even sadder and more alone.

3　He hadn't realised that he had been unconscious for a while.
4　He thought 'the gold' was his money.
5　The words are 'soft, warm curls'.
6　He wanted to check that it wasn't a dream.
7　The words are 'old quiverings of tenderness'.
8　He can't comprehend that there may be a natural cause to explain the arrival of the child.

Summary

The little girl reminds Silas of his sister, both in her physical shape and in the rather old and dirty clothes she is wearing. He used to carry his sister about in his arms until she died as a young child. Thinking of her revived the normal emotion of tenderness, which he had stifled in Raveloe, and also the feelings of respect and amazement that God was controlling his destiny.
(70 words)

Vocabulary

(These answers are only examples)
a)　It was really senseless being rude to the boss; now you'll lose your job. (= a stupid action)
b)　That was sensible of you to do so much preparation for the exam; now you've got a grade A pass. (= a wise action)
c)　Be careful what you say; Mary is so sensitive she'll burst into tears if she thinks you're criticising her.
d)　I've got some sensational news! I've just heard that Prince Edward is getting married to a chorus girl!
e)　He couldn't explain why, but some kind of sixth sense warned him not to sail on the *Titanic* in 1912.
f)　Elizabeth was going to hitch-hike round the world by herself, but she finally came to her senses when her father explained the dangers involved.

Idioms

1 e　2 f　3 b　4 c　5 a　6 d

Unit 7 *Return of the Native*

Understanding and Appreciating

1　Since Mrs Yeobright had refused to attend the wedding, Eustacia hardly expected to be visited by her.
2　She means that she was acting in Clym's best interests, rather than merely being against Eustacia.
3　'It' refers to the fact that Clym and Eustacia are now married, and therefore Mrs Yeobright can't change the situation.
4　Eustacia feels that she comes from a better social background than Clym, and that it should not be implied that she has done well by marrying him.
5　She had not expected to be living in such a wild, remote place.
6　She is implying that Eustacia might have used deception to encourage Clym to marry her.
7　It shows that she is clearly angry and embarrassed by the implication of deception.
8　She is referring to her supposed eagerness in marrying Clym.

Summary

When Eustacia is asked by Mrs Yeobright if she has received money from Mr Wildeve, she assumes that Mrs Yeobright is implying that she is still maintaining a relationship with him. Eustacia does not realise that Mrs Yeobright is talking about money intended for Clym. Eustacia is angry with Mrs Yeobright, partly for having been against her before her marriage, but mainly for implying that she is immoral and that she is trying to turn Clym against his own mother.
(80 words)

Vocabulary

Affection	a) 1	b) 3	c) 2
Anger	a) 3	b) 1	c) 2
Surprise	a) 3	b) 2	c) 1

Idioms

1 d　2 e　3 b　4 a　5 f　6 c

Unit 8 *The First Men in the Moon*

Understanding and Appreciating

1 Cavor feels sorry for Bedford, and blames himself for encouraging Bedford to accompany him.
2 Cavor felt that Bedford would have led a successful life on Earth.
3 Bedford felt that he had put a lot of effort into the planning, especially concerning the practical aspects of its construction.
4 It is very matter-of-fact; there is no sign of emotion, only the words 'we arrived'.
5 It affected his personality, causing him to make quick, unwise decisions, and to become argumentative.
6 It was madness to eat the vesicles, because they caused Bedford and Cavor to become drunk, which made it easier for them to be captured.
7 He comments on their tolerance, since they could have killed him out of revenge.
8 Cavor thinks Bedford must have been trying to get back to Earth before him, and presumably to gain prestige just for himself.

Summary

After Bedford had killed three of the Selenites, they both tried to escape, forcing their way through a number of these creatures and killing seven or eight more. On reaching the exterior, Bedford and Cavor separated in order to try and find the sphere. Cavor was chased by some more Selenites, including two who looked rather different, and was eventually recaptured after falling into a crevasse and injuring himself.
(69 words)

Vocabulary

1 e 2 g 3 a 4 h 5 b 6 d 7 f 8 c

Idioms

1 b 2 d 3 a 4 f 5 c 6 h 7 g 8 e

Unit 9 *A Room With a View*

Understanding and Appreciating

1 She should not have given them rooms without a view.
2 The whole atmosphere in the hotel is English, as are most of the guests.
3 Miss Bartlett feels under an obligation to Lucy, as her mother has paid part of her expenses.
4 They don't expect a stranger to shout across the room and take part in their conversation.
5 It was because, in her society, it was not customary to speak to strangers until one had had long enough to assess them.
6 It means before everything gets established, and relationships and arrangements have been made.
7 She is trying to discourage him from continuing the conversation.
8 They are shocked by what they consider to be ill-bred behaviour, and feel sorry that anyone of their class should be subjected to it.

Summary

Miss Bartlett and Lucy had booked rooms with a view of the River Arno, and were disappointed to find that they had been given rooms looking onto a courtyard instead. The reason why they did not accept the old man's offer was that such offers would not have been made or accepted in their society, especially in such a public and embarrassing manner. They also do not want to feel under an obligation to someone they consider to be 'ill-bred'.
(80 words)

Vocabulary

1 g 2 e 3 a 4 h 5 c 6 d 7 f 8 b

Phrasal Verbs (get)

1 c 2 d 3 a 4 h 5 g 6 b 7 e 8 f

Unit 10 *Sons and Lovers*

Famous People

1 c   2 e   3 d   4 a   5 b

Understanding and Appreciating

1   It is the unusually excited way in which his mother is reacting to the letter.
2   It shows that she feels deeply involved in her son's achievement, and that they have done it together.
3   He means that he is very impressed.
4   Paul is afraid that his mother has made a mistake and he does not want to be disappointed.
5   They are both in an emotional state, and they argue about the amount to help to relieve the stress.
6   He had hoped the story was true about the prize being fifty pounds.
7   He does not feel that the painting was worth so much money.
8   Mrs Morrel is described as trying not to notice the evidence of coal-mining on her husband's hands and face.

Summary

Mrs Morrel is thrilled by the fact that Paul's artistic effort has been rewarded with public recognition. She is not interested in the prize-money itself, but is delighted simply with the achievement. Mr Morrel, on the other hand, is only interested in the amount of money Paul has won, and in how soon he will receive it. It never occurs to him to be proud of the fact that he has won a competition.
(74 words)

Vocabulary

Fear a) 2 b) 1   c) 3   Joy a) 2   b) 3   c) 1   Sadness a) 3   b) 2   c) 1

Phrasal Verbs (put)

1 up with   2 aside   3 in for   4 out   5 off   6 down to   7 across   8 off

Unit 11 *1984*

Understanding and Appreciating

1   It would be impossible to utter non-party thoughts, since the words would not exist to express them.
2   The 'A vocabulary' was much smaller and more limited in meaning.
3   It was constructed for the expression of concrete thoughts, and anything of a theoretical nature was not possible.
4   It took more words to express the same meaning in Oldspeak, and caused a loss of the desired political overtones as well.
5   It implies that it is good to think in the manner expected by the state.
6   It is because it is limited to scientific and technical words, and will therefore not be used in everyday situations.
7   These would be any meanings which were not considered desirable by the state.
8   It would prevent any exchanges or discussion between scientists, and would therefore limit them to their own, small sphere.

Summary

The 'A vocabulary' consisted of simple words to be used in everyday situations. Each word could only express one idea, and there was no possibility of any ambiguity or difference in meaning. The 'B vocabulary' consisted of words intended for political purposes. They not only had a particular political implication, but were actually intended to force the speaker to think in the desired manner.
(64 words)

Vocabulary

1   The writer was neutral.

Unit 12 *Lord of the Flies*

Understanding and Appreciating

1   Sam and Eric still react in the civilised way they have been brought up, and can't quite believe what is going on.
2   It emphasises the fact that they have become like primitive savages.
3   It indicates threat or menace.
4   Jack realises that if he does not establish his leadership at this moment, he will have lost the chance for ever.
5   It is when they see that the fight is going to be interrupted by Piggy's speech.
6   Roger finally gives up any of his previously-held, civilised, restraining feelings, and whole-heartedly enjoys the act of violence he is committing.
7   It symbolises the final and complete breaking of the civilised and democratic society originally formed on the island.
8   The first is where it states that he had 'no time for even a grunt', and the second is when the twitching of his arms and legs is described as 'like a pig's after it has been killed'.

Summary

Piggy tries to bring the boys back to their civilised ways, reminding them of the function of the conch, and telling them they are acting like irresponsible children. He tries to contrast being sensible and having law and order (and, ultimately, being rescued) with savage behaviour, hunting and killing. His appeal is unsuccessful, because he has not realised the extent to which the hunters have become like savages, and that an appeal to their civilized instincts is now useless.
(79 words)

Vocabulary

1 clans   2 race   3 band   4 crowds   5 troop   6 class   7 generation   8 society

Phrasal Verbs (work)

1 b   2 e   3 d   4 a   5 c

Unit 13 *Room at the Top*

Understanding and Appreciating

1   He contrasts it with the black background of the buildings.
2   She clearly does not mean what she says, as she holds out her face for a kiss at the same time.
3   It has to refer to the cinema, as the next phrase refers to the theatre.
4   She feels it implies being alone, where they could hold and kiss one another.
5   He feels so happy because he is so much in love with Susan.
6   It clearly has the same meaning as 'masters' and 'overlords', and refers to the bosses.
7   It makes it clear that they have only been window-shopping, and have not really bought those items at all.
8   It gives the effect of Susan's non-stop chatter; she follows one remark with another and another.

Summary

Talking about foreign holidays would normally cause resentment in these circumstances because the people listening have not got enough money to afford expensive holidays like that. It does not do so in this case, however, because Susan is so natural in the way she talks about her holidays and is clearly not trying to show off or to give the impression of being above everyone else.
(66 words)

Vocabulary 1

(This is a suggested answer)

Positive	Negative	Neutral
determined	ruthless	persistent*
ambitious	selfish	sensitive*
energetic		precise*
reliable		

*These depend on how you feel about them. Make a good case to support your views!

Vocabulary 2

1 gossiping   2 have words   3 addressed   4 discuss   5 debate   6 babbling   7 have a word
8 lectures

Unit 14 *The Jewel in the Crown*

Understanding and Appreciating

1   It was because the children now saw her in the role of a heroine, and were half-expecting her to perform another heroic deed.
2   She was promoted to a post where she was in charge of a school.
3   The implication is that the painting is not a true reflection of the real situation in India, but that dirty, messy beggars would not enhance the image of the British Empire.
4   It might be offensive to the Indian people to appear too proud of the fact that India was British.
5   She had used it for teaching purposes.
6   The junior school had suffered through lack of attention because he devoted most of his time to the older boys.
7   The British might have intended to do good, but did not necessarily do so. On reflection, therefore, Miss Crane changes 'benevolence' to 'good intentions'.
8   He was an intellectual man, and thought God could be served by using his mind, rather than by being of practical help to people who were suffering.

Summary

The 'semi-historical' aspect of the painting is that in which it depicts the moment in British history when the Queen of Britain also received the title of Empress of India. The 'semi-allegorical' aspect concerns the title of the painting. 'The jewel in her crown' is not the gem being carried by the prince, but is India herself, the most important and precious part of the Empire.
(66 words)

Vocabulary

1 c   2 e   3 h   4 g   5 a   6 d   7 b   8 f

Idioms

1 c   2 f   3 e   4 a   5 b   6 d

Unit 15 *Hotel du Lac*

Understanding and Appreciating

1   This was the period before travel agents organised package holidays on a large scale.
2   Good staff were attracted by the hotel's professional reputation.
3   The hotel does not want to offer the sort of amenities which would make it popular with modern-day tourists.
4   New clients were attracted by the personal recommendations of their friends who had already stayed at the hotel.
5   It would be if you needed to get away from your normal life or to escape public attention for a while.
6   Guests expect the hotel to have high standards, but at the hotel it was assumed that the guests themselves would have similar high standards and behave accordingly.
7   Because of its quietness, people like doctors or solicitors made a note of it, in case they needed somewhere to send patients for a rest or had clients who needed privacy for some reason.
8   It implies that most tourists go off to the popular resorts without thinking for themselves, whereas a discerning traveller chooses to stay at the Hotel du Lac.

Summary

Life in the hotel was very quiet, with very little to see or do there. There was a bar, but it was small and dark and was therefore not somewhere guests felt comfortable. During the first part of the morning, chambermaids made the beds and did the cleaning, but were then not seen again until the evening when they came in to tidy the rooms and turn down the beds.
(70 words)

Vocabulary 1

1 f   2 d   3 g   4 b   5 h   6 c   7 a   8 e

Vocabulary 2

1 g   2 f   3 h   4 e   5 a   6 b   7 d   8 c

Index to exercises

Vocabulary

Idioms

Phrasal verbs